SHE LOSES ALL

AN ARTEMIS BLYTHE MYSTERY THRILLER

GEORGIA WAGNER

CONTENTS

PROLOGUE:

Gabbie Donovan didn't mean to break the old gate.

But the rusted barb snapped nonetheless, coming off in a shower of red dust.

She blinked rapidly, waving a hand in front of her face to hold back a sneeze. One hand remained braced against the top of the fence, the other gripped at a twisted, black support pole.

"Psst!" her friend, Clay, whispered from the other side of the fence. "Careful—you'll spook the ghosts."

She stiffened, half-clambered over the fence but now feeling some amount of resistance at this comment. "That's not funny," she whispered back.

Bright teeth flashed in the dark, displaying a Colgate smile. Clay hastened back towards her, extending a hand to help her over the barrier.

With some air of reluctance, she accepted the offered hand, though, inwardly, her heart pounded.

The two of them had been in the same class for nearly five months, ever since her family had moved to St. Charles. It was her last year of high school, and he had been one of the few friendly faces.

It helped that he was nice to look at.

His hand was warm and also covered in dust from the fence.

She dropped on the other side of the encircling, black barricade, outside the historic home situated in a large double lot facing the Fox River.

The scent of the water lingered on the air. If she went quiet and listened closely, she thought she could hear the murmur and burble of the current rushing by.

Gabbie glanced past her partner in crime and looked up at the old mansion sitting on the top of a grassy hill. Large windows overlooked the lawn and the river beyond. The house itself was half brick and half stucco, painted purple, as if the architect had given up halfway through.

Gabbie felt a strange tingle along her arms thanks to a passing zephyr.

The wind coming over the river brought with it a fresh scent of vegetation and water. But another scent, rising from the ground and spreading from the direction of the mansion, competed with this odor.

Mold and rot from water damage hung on the air.

Gabbie stared at the historic home, swallowing as she did. She tried to keep the tremble from her voice as she said, "Are you sure this is a good idea?"

Clay grinned at her again, flashing that same smile that had enticed her into this trip in the first place. Technically, this wasn't a date. But they were hanging out one on one, and her friends would never have let her hear the end of it if she turned down the opportunity of spending time with the star of the lacrosse team.

Other friends warned her about Clay. He only wants one thing, they said.

And Gabbie wasn't stupid. She knew the type. But she wasn't sure she minded. As a new girl coming into a strange schooling situation, it had been hard to make friends. Harder still to keep them. Her family was placing roots in the area, setting roots in the community.

A little bit of fun with Clay Johnson was a low price to pay to make up for her complete lack of reputation.

She shivered again. "It's not really haunted," she said, still whispering.

"Are you asking me or telling me?"

She frowned at him. "It's not."

"Okay," he said. "Then let's go inside."

The two of them stood on the grassy lawn, which was maintained by caretakers.

But Gabbie's legs felt rooted to the spot; she shot a look over her shoulder, through the fence, watching the moon reflect off the rippling water.

"Are you sure no one saw us?"

He frowned at her now, his million-dollar smile fading like a sunrise behind thick cloud cover. "I thought you were down to have some fun."

She instantly retorted, "I am." Then, to prove the point, she began to march up the sloping grass towards the old house.

It was just a stupid structure after all. She'd been in big homes before; in fact, her father's last house, though about a century newer, had also been three stories.

She exhaled faintly but kept her breathing in check, eyes fixed determinedly on the front steps.

She wouldn't go inside. Just up the stairs, maybe to knock on the door then run.

That would have to satisfy her would-be beau.

For his part, he was smiling less and moving more quietly the closer they got to the mansion.

He had been the one to suggest the place was haunted and had been teasing her on the walk over here, as they had met at the school. Gabbie didn't want to think what her parents would say if they found out she had lied about the afterschool study session.

And now, she was beginning to wonder if Clay really was the prize that social media posts might suggest.

The old, moldy, worn-down house stood out like a mausoleum. She had just learned that word in social studies. Mausoleum. A fancy tomb.

She reached the bottom step, her feet pressing against the old wood. It creaked under the pressure, and she took a shaky step onto the next stair to earn another groaning protest of wood. Another step. This time, she braced herself with a hand outstretched against a splintered rail.

The wood was rough beneath her fingertips. She withdrew her hand, wincing and remembering when she had gotten a splinter from a 2B pencil while practicing her sketches.

"All right," she said as they reached the door. "We did it. You happy?"

She received no response.

She scowled and turned to glare at Clay. "Did you hear—"

Clay was nowhere to be seen.

She went quiet and felt a prickle along her shoulders.

She swallowed and took a hesitant step down the stairs again.

4

But now, presenting her back to the door of the haunted house only made her feel more uncomfortable. She shot a glance over her shoulder, and like this, crab shuffling, she sidestepped down the stairs again.

"Clay?" she whispered, her voice trembling once more. "Clay, where are you?" she said, a bit louder, trying to choose between fear and fury. Was he trying to pull a prank?

"If you think this is funny..." she said, putting iron to her voice. But it sounded more brittle than that, like frail ice.

"Clay Johnson, you come out here this instant!"

And then the door behind her creaked.

She stiffened and shot a sharp look over her shoulder. The wind seemed to have calmed momentarily. Even the scent of the water faded.

Or perhaps that was just because she forgot to breathe.

She stared through a gap in the open door. There came a faint creaking sound.

She stood frozen on the stairs. Every instinct in her screamed for her to run.

But she couldn't move. Sheer panic like she had never felt before glued her feet to the ground. Even if she could scream, the historic home wasn't just on a double lot but was adjacent to an old church which was unoccupied this late at night.

And then she felt a hand on her shoulder.

Fingers against her skin.

She nearly leapt off the stairs over the railing.

She screamed, whirling around, hands raising to defend herself. And she found herself staring at the grinning face of Clay Johnson. He was laughing now, bent double, clutching at his stomach, and giggling.

She realized now that he had ducked out of sight over the rail, hiding behind the wooden banister.

She was gasping, sweat pockmarking her forehead.

"That's not funny!" she snapped. "That's not funny at all!"

But he was still laughing, shaking horribly. He clutched at his stomach, his face turning interesting hues. "You should have seen yourself," he said, giggling. "Oh my gosh, I can't even believe it. That was hilarious."

She glared but he didn't seem to care.

That's when she heard the creaking sound again.

"Hush, be quiet," she said suddenly.

He was still laughing, shaking his head side to side and pulling his phone out from his pocket. "Man, I wish I had videoed you. That was classic."

"I said be quiet," she repeated, more fervently.

He glared at her. "No need to get pushy, jeez. Calm down. It was just a joke."

But her eyes widened, and she held a finger to her lips. "I hear something."

He rolled his eyes. "Ha, ha, very funny."

But she gave another urgent shake of her head, glancing back through the door. Another quiet creaking sound.

He went still as well. Clay frowned. "Wait, what was that?"

"See," she insisted. "You hear it too."

He hesitated but then nodded once. He took a step up the stairs, joining her and peering through the open door.

"What is that?" he whispered.

He wasn't pointing at the door, though, but rather was indicating...

She followed his finger and spotted it as well.

A thin glaze of red spread across the porch, under the door, coming from the direction of the atrium.

She stared.

"That is *not* funny. You're sick. Is that James? Get out here, James!"

But Clay clutched at her arm. "Be quiet. No one's in there. That's not Jay."

She stared and then looked towards the door again. Again, she felt a strong urge to turn tail and run.

But her father was a doctor.

He had brought her up to help people if they were in danger. And that thin veneer on the ground certainly looked like blood. What if someone was injured? What if someone was hurt?

He was tugging at her arm now, though. "Let's get out of here."

"What if someone's in there?" she said.

"I don't care, let's go."

"No, hang on. What is that?"

She spotted something now, beneath the staircase; she could just make out the curling banister that led up to the stairs inside the atrium. And beneath it, the chandelier was dangling—but it was a very oddly shaped chandelier...

Actually, as she stared, she wasn't so sure that... it... was...

The floor creaked as she reached the top of the porch and reached out, pushing the door slowly open. And then she stared. A scream caught in her throat.

Behind her, Clay cursed, and she heard the sound of pounding feet as he sprinted away. Which left her standing there, staring into the open door.

There was a body on the ground, bleeding, and above the body, a second corpse. This one hanged by rope, arms limp at its side like iron pendulums dangling uselessly towards the ground. Face distorted and bulging above the taut, bristling noose.

The body swung slowly, creaking with each motion. The rope twisted above, lashed to the banister.

1

It was as she stood in the airport that Artemis Blythe received the call.

Cynthia Washington. One of Artemis' favorite chess analysts.

"Hello?"

The first sound she heard was sobbing. Artemis hesitated, her mismatched eyes—one blue and one hazel—darting between the announcement board over the baggage-check counter and her phone. Her flight was in an hour. She was finally leaving the Pacific Northwest, returning to her small apartment in Salinas, California.

"Umm—hello?" Artemis tried again, feeling a jolt of anxiety. She took a few steps away from the queue in front of the check-in counter. The familiar scent of airports lingered. Part stale coffee, part body odor and part anxiety.

Artemis had far more than her share of this last item.

She could feel a knot forming in her stomach, oftentimes a harbinger of a coming panic attack if she wasn't careful. Along with suits, dresses and driving, airports were also on a list of things she hated.

The sobbing continued, but a voice came through, stuttering, gasping. "A-Artemis? I-is that you?"

"Mrs. Washington, what's wrong?" Artemis said, frowning. She moved further back, away from the queue, standing in the shadow of a giant, rectangular support column now with a banner welcoming travelers to Seattle. The printed photograph on the banner displayed a scene of misty mountains and forests above a second photo of a seemingly floating bridge across expansive, blue water.

"I—I... he's dead..." Cynthia whispered, her voice squeaking.

Artemis felt her blood go cold. "Who's dead? Mrs. Washington, what happened?"

"Henry... he... he's dead."

"Henry?" Artemis felt her throat constrict, her eyes widening. She pictured Mrs. Washington's smiling-eyed husband. Pictured the number of online calls she'd had with the two where they often sat on their favorite, pink couch, beneath a corkboard covered in photographs of their grandchildren.

Both the Washingtons were piercingly smart. Each of them an international master in their own right, though, they no longer competed in most tournaments. They were the first analysts to ever look over a game of hers that she'd posted online, nearly a decade ago. They were honest, blunt... but often kind in their delivery, and she loved them for it.

The idea that Cynthia had lost her best friend—a forty-year marriage—was a gut punch.

"N-not *my* Henry," she said. "Well..." She was panting now, still trying to console herself. "Well, yes... my Henry. But not my husband."

Artemis felt a spurt of relief then instantly felt guilty. Still, she found she could breathe at least a little easier, though, her long-time friend was clearly still very distraught.

"What happened? Who died?"

"My grandson. Henry Rodine." Cynthia was breathing easier now, but her voice was still shaking. Artemis' fingers clenched tightly on the phone while also hefting her carry-on in her other hand. "He... he hanged himself. Or... well, that's what the police say."

Artemis decided not to reply this time, simply listening. She'd often been a student of human behavior. Sometimes compassion, under-standing, would shine a light on emotion. Right now, though, she wanted information. Clearly, Cynthia had called for a reason, and if Artemis was going to help, she needed to know *what* she was helping with.

And so she remained silent, biting her lip, feeling a swirl of sec-ond-hand grief and anxiety. She didn't cry, nor did she tear up. Artemis hadn't cried in nearly fifteen years. She didn't remember how, and, even with the help of multiple psychologists, psychiatrists, counselors and coaches, she'd never been able to uncork the tears.

But that didn't mean she didn't feel grief, and now it was coming in the form of white-hot lances of anxiety through her stomach on behalf of her friend.

Cynthia continued, taking Artemis' silence as a cue. "He... they say he... Oh God, it's so horrible. They say he *killed* his girlfriend. Then hanged himself." The woman, who was in her sixties, broke into another series of sobbing.

Artemis noticed someone with a green backpack waving in her direction. One of the other passengers who'd been standing in line and trying to hold her spot. Artemis winced, nodding politely in gratitude but shooing away the help. She turned her shoulder, clearly indicating she was busy. Body-language was often more accurate than verbal communication in Artemis' experience. She shot a final look of thanks with a wince and then stepped around the support column, standing between the large, painted concrete pillar and a window facing a gray street.

"I'm so very, very sorry," Artemis murmured. "I can't even imagine." This wasn't *strictly* true. Artemis' own upbringing had familiarized her with homicidal family members. But she continued, "Is there anything I can do?"

She'd meant it to be rhetorical.

But Mrs. Washington instantly said, "Yes! Oh, dear God, thank you—yes! Please. I... I wouldn't ask." The woman swallowed. "I wouldn't ask, but Henry... my husband, he was very close with our grandson. And he's locked himself up in our room. He refuses to eat." She sobbed again. "Refuses to sleep. And I'm just so, so scared, Artemis."

Artemis made a gentle, calming sound. "That's horrible. I don't even know what to say. But..." She hesitated, trying to think what to add next. Artemis knew that women were accused of *only* having emotions. Conventional wisdom often said they weren't interested in *solutions* so much as being heard. And while Artemis respected the conventional advice, she hadn't always found it to be true in her own dealings.

To her, solutions mattered.

Emotions often ended in panic attacks. Solutions mastered those.

And so, she said, carefully, "What... what precisely can I help you with, Mrs. Washington?"

If her friend needed someone to talk to for an hour, then Artemis would happily stay on the line. But she also knew Cynthia... something else was going on. Something that the older woman wasn't saying yet.

Mrs. Washington cleared her throat, paused delicately. Then said, slowly, her voice going lower, softer, as if she were whispering, scared she might be overheard. "He didn't do it," she said firmly.

"I see."

"No, wait. I know you think everyone says that. But he didn't do it, Artemis. I swear it to you. Henry... Henry was troubled. And... and yes, a few years ago he had some issues, but he was turning things around. He was getting *better*! He wouldn't do this. Couldn't do this!"

Again, Artemis didn't say anything, prompting further information.

"And... And..." Cynthia released a long, pent-up sigh, suggesting they were finally arriving at the exact and precise reason for the call. "I know you've..." she swallowed. "You've had some experience in the past... helping the FBI. And... and I was wondering if you'd be willing to help us." She said this last part very quickly, like ripping off a band-aid. And this time, though a silence ensued, Cynthia didn't keep speaking. The two of them went quiet, both breathing into their microphones.

Artemis was dumbfounded. Not because she was prompting further response, but because she felt like she'd been hit by a train. Her mind was spinning now. The scent of stale-coffee was joined by the faint odor of gasoline as the sliding, glass doors in the front of the airport opened and closed, allowing a gust of cool air to sweep the fragrance of the idling taxis and shuttles through the vestibule.

"Artemis?" Cynthia said tentatively. "Are you... are you still there?"

Artemis swallowed. "Umm, yeah. Yes, Mrs. Washington, sorry. J ust..." She trailed off, wincing. "Was there an investigation already, ma'am?"

"Yes! Yes, no, but wait! They didn't believe us. All they saw was the report from his school, some of the run-ins he'd had a few years ago. Small things. A bit of shoplifting, some bullying at the school. But he'd turned his life around. He really had! He was studying hard. He *loved* Paige."

"Paige was his girlfriend?"

A sob that sounded something like *yes!*

"I see... I... Mrs. Washington, I don't work for the FBI. You know that, right?"

"Yes! But you've been helping them, right? That's what you asked me and Henry to look at on Monday, wasn't it? The postcards?"

Artemis bit her lip. Cynthia was right. Those postcards had been sent to her father by an ex-con named Baker. They were written in code though, and Artemis *still* couldn't figure out what they said. In fact, trying to decipher them was starting to detract from restful sleep.

"It was... I'm not sure what I can do, though," Artemis said slowly.

"Henry and his girlfriend were found in an old historic building on the Fox River!" Cynthia said urgently, pressing her case. "The crime scene is easily accessible. You... you have an eye for details, Artemis. I'm begging you," she said, her voice cracking again.

"No, no, don't beg, please." Artemis winced, glancing around the edge of the support column towards the screen of departures. Her eyes landed on her flight, halfway down the list. Moving across to the small notification. *On-time.*

Her hand shifted its grip on her carry-on, which held her laptop—the most precious cargo of an online chess streamer. She didn't even have a change of clothing anymore. She'd thrown away a few of the items back in her hotel room, and a new set would be waiting for her back in Salinas. Artemis often ordered her clothes online—not from clothing stores but online retailers that boasted baggy shirts and sweatpants that fit all. Artemis' slim frame was often smaller than intended for such ensembles, but she simply couldn't be bothered.

There were those in the chess community who resented her symmetrical features, cherubic nose and coal-black hair framing porcelain skin. She didn't think of herself as pretty, but some of her online detractors did, and in response, Artemis dressed simply. She didn't wear makeup. Didn't wear jewelry. Used soap instead of perfume. Her dark hair was often found pulled back in a simple ponytail.

She missed the sunshine. Missed the fair weather. Missed, most of all, the feeling of having Pinelake in her rearview mirror. The only thing keeping her had been an offer from Agent Grant to train with the FBI—a preliminary thing, mostly. But Artemis still had three days before Grant required an answer, and she needed to clear her head.

Besides, the mid-season online blitz tournament had extended a last-minute invitation. Apparently, Anton Radesh, the current world champion, would be participating. Because of Artemis' online presence, the tournament had—last minute—asked her to join.

There were so many things on her plate. Even Jamie Kramer had called her last night. She'd missed the call, and he hadn't left a voicemail, but it was eating at her to know what her old sweetheart wanted.

And yet, as the reasons piled up for her to refuse...

Artemis could still hear her friend's shaky breathing. Could hear the pain in Mrs. Washington's voice. By the sound of things, the police had already ruled it a murder-suicide.

Artemis didn't have access to casefiles, crime-scene reports.

Her life was one tinged in death... It followed her wherever she went, it seemed.

Did she really want to step back into its clutches? Even for a friend? She thought of what her sister, Helen, used to say. *Choice is stronger than blood.* Helen had been full of tactical and strategic advice growing up. But this particular saying of hers had been deeper, meant more. Choice is stronger than blood.

Helen was gone now. There were rumors, hints, whispers that she was still alive out there. But where? How? Artemis didn't know... She would have given *everything* to have another week with her sister. Would have given up chess, the financial success that was starting, the recognition she was beginning to get on the circuit.

She would have given it all away for Helen.

But Helen was gone. Artemis didn't really have a family any more. Her father was in prison, her brother neck-deep in the Seattle mob.

The Washingtons had been the next best thing.

By choice.

Artemis let out a shaking breath. Then said, quietly, "I can't promise anything. But I'll be there this evening."

2

It was closer to the depths of night when Artemis stepped out of Chicago O'Hare Airport onto the gray sidewalk. Rescheduling her flight and changing her ticket had been a headache. Then her flight had been delayed.

Now, though, as she moved through the sliding, glass doors outside the Windy City, Artemis released a breath of her own to join the predominant air current.

She looked up and down the terminals, glancing past where figures huddled with their bags on trolleys or waved at cars that hit their blinkers and tried to double-park within yellow lines.

Artemis pulled her phone from her pocket, feeling the tension in her stomach growing as she stood in the unfamiliar terminal outside the unfamiliar city.

She'd never been to Chicago before. She rarely traveled. Illinois, to her, wasn't just a so-called flyover state. It was simply trivia on a map.

Until today.

Now, she shifted uncomfortably, holding her carry-on with her laptop and realizing she'd have to order some new clothes and rush the shipping if she wanted anything clean to wear. She didn't *know* how long any of this would take.

Her phone vibrated as she turned it back on. She knew phones could be put on an Airplane mode. But she hadn't wanted to risk it, so she'd turned it off completely.

As she glanced at her notifications, which included a stream of information on the most recent chess news, she frowned.

Another missed call.

Jamie Kramer had tried to reach out again. And this time she had a voicemail.

Hesitantly, her teeth pressed against her lower lip, she shot a quick text message to Mrs. Washington, who'd said she would be waiting in the cellphone parking lot for Artemis to arrive. *Arrived. Terminal 2D.*

Artemis double-checked, glancing at the blue sign over her head and then lifted her phone, standing on the sidewalk and trying to avoid any of the other passengers and commuters streaming past her.

She heard slamming doors, gasping as men tried to heft *too-heavy* bags into the back of waiting vehicles. And then, her voicemail recording declared. *You have* ONE *new message.*

She waited, heard the telling silence, and then, Jamie's voice.

Instantly, she felt like he sounded nervous and sleep deprived. Not that she could blame him. Almost two weeks ago, his mother had been murdered by his own father. And then his father had been shot by an FBI agent.

Artemis shivered at the memory. She'd been there at the time, though, Jamie wouldn't know that.

Hey... the voicemail started. *Been a bit. Sorry for ghosting you there... Just, been taking care of Sophie. Moving into the new place. Umm...*

yeah... you know... all of this, it's kinda put things in perspective. I mean, shit... I almost feel like you must have... Not—not trying to be rude. Just, you know. You get it. With your old man, with... with all of it. A long sigh, a swallow. *Well, just seeing how you're doing, I guess... I don't really... really know who to talk to, you know? Don't really know—ah, well, whatever. Hang on—What's up, Sophie?* His voice became muffled as he held a small conversation in the background, suggesting he'd lowered his device. A few seconds later, he raised the phone again. *Shit,* he said. *Do you know anything about dinosaurs... God, she's in first grade! But...* Another sigh. It wasn't a sigh of resignation; more like... determination. The exhausted sound of a man on a path with no options. He ended with, *But yeah... was good seeing you. I don't... I don't hold against you... Not that I would, but, well, whatever. Anyway—talk to you later—Sophie's calling again.*

And then the voicemail went silent.

Artemis frowned, wrinkling her forehead. She could feel the same lancing sensation in her stomach, and part of her wanted to immediately call him back. But when she checked the time, it was nearly nine PM, already. By the sound of things, Jamie had his hands busy and would need some sleep.

If he was taking care of his seven-year-old sister now, it meant that he was probably going to be the one to drive her to school as well.

"No... Better to text or something..." she murmured out loud to herself.

Before she could think of what to say, though, she heard a faint, little beep of a horn. She glanced up and watched as a bright, pink Toyota Prius pulled in between two larger SUVs waiting at the curb of Terminal 2.

A hand was flapping out the window. She recognized the cheerful wave, though, it had lost some of its usual gusto.

The window rolled down, revealing a smiling face. The smile seemed somewhat fixed but very intentional. Mrs. Washington was the sort that smiled not so much to express emotion as to comfort others.

A lot of what Mrs. Washington did was for others.

Artemis waved back, forcing a smile of her own. One thing she noticed immediately. The passenger seat was empty. Henry hadn't come with his wife.

Artemis had never seen the analysts separated before. In fact, she'd never seen them *in person* before. She'd often wanted to, but her aversion to travel had prevented it. And now... under these circumstances, it was a very strange experience.

Still, she hefted her bag and approached the car.

She heard the soft *click* of locks and opened the passenger side door. As she slipped into the car, Mrs. Washington exclaimed, "Artemis! Oh Lord, look at you—you're even prettier in person."

Artemis' left cheek dimpled as she gave a quick and polite nod. "Thank you," she murmured. "And you're as lovely as ever. I love your earrings."

Cynthia gave a little laugh, this one sounding genuine. She nodded, her large, golden, hoop earrings swishing. The woman's pale hair was cut short, perfectly complementing her dark skin. She had wrinkles in the corners of her eyes, suggesting a habit of smiling.

She was also much smaller than Artemis had expected. Though perhaps that was because the last person to drive Artemis around a city had been six-foot-four.

She thought vaguely of Agent Cameron Forester.

But she shook her head, refocusing. She closed the door, buckled and then turned sideways to face her friend fully. "Is Henry still back home?"

She nodded quickly. "He still won't eat," she said, swallowing. "Won't come out of his room."

Artemis nodded once.

Someone was beeping their horn behind them, though, and Mrs. Washington slowly guided her vehicle back into the flow of the street, moving away from the terminals.

Artemis glanced at the clock on the dash. She considered her options for a moment. This wasn't a social call. There wasn't established etiquette where this sort of thing was concerned.

But the pitch on the phone had been the crime scene.

An old, historic home on the Fox River. The site, according to the police, of a murder-suicide. The place where Mrs. Washington's oldest grandson had been killed.

If there was any spot to start, it would be the historic house.

Plus, this late at night... police presence and nosy neighbors would be at a minimum.

Artemis chewed on her lower lip, shifting in her seat and tugging at her seatbelt, watching the road flash by as they picked up pace, heading away from the airport.

She couldn't really believe what she was thinking but also couldn't think of an alternative.

She'd agreed.

She'd said she would help.

Not that there was much she thought she could do. Artemis hadn't even been able to find a news article online yet.

"When did this happen?" Artemis said, shooting a sidelong glance.

"Late last night," Mrs. Washington murmured. "That's what's so frustrating. They already closed the investigation. Said there *isn't* an investigation." She shook her head in frustration. "I'm a God-fearing woman, Artemis, but it's enough to make a woman wonder if my little

21

grandbaby is just a statistic to them..." She trailed off, biting her lip. She sobbed then shook her head. "No... No, no, I'm not going to say it." She forced a smile and a nod.

But Artemis was frowning now. Her friend was clearly in pain. Her response was a desire to help—this wasn't *quite* the same as courage, but it was a close facsimile.

She nodded once. "Alright—let's go to the crime scene. Would that be okay?" She hesitated, though. "Umm... Does... does your husband have a car, too?"

"No, why?"

Artemis didn't want to mention that driving a bright pink Prius to trespass at a crime-scene might attract the wrong sorts of attention. But then she just shook her head, trying to think what Agent Forester would do.

"We can park the street over." Artemis nodded once, reaching a conclusion.

Their brightly hued vehicle picked up pace. A small, waste bin sat neatly in the center console. Above it, a foam cut-out shaped like a tulip emitted a scent like roses. A pile of wrapped mints was wedged into a coin tray beneath the unused cigarette burner, and a little, golden crucifix with beads swayed beneath the mirror. Artemis glanced out of the window at a bridge whipping by overhead in a blur of gray. Her tone turned solemn.

"Do you think I could ask you a few questions, please?"

Cynthia adjusted the rearview mirror and then shot a look at Artemis. Her expression was still gentle, but the smile was gone as she said, "What do you want to know? I'm an open book."

Artemis nodded. "Can you tell me a little bit about your grandson?"

Mrs. Washington inhaled slowly, as if calming herself and then she began to talk. But now, Artemis recognized the way her favorite analyst chose to deliver information. On the phone, she had been grieving, in pain, and scared; now, though, following a couple of shaky inhales, she recited information as if running through the annotation of Artemis' latest match.

She spoke quickly, in curt, clear sentences, enunciating the words. She spoke slowly enough to be understood but quick enough to suggest not only did she have an acrobatic tongue, but she was holding back to allow Artemis to process the information. "Henry is our oldest grandson. We have eight. He was born to my eldest daughter."

"And you have three kids?"

"Yes. Rebeka, Ashley and Abraham."

"You mentioned Henry was getting into some trouble a few years ago."

"Henry's father isn't in the picture, and he had a difficult time in school for a while. As I mentioned, he started getting into petty theft, shoplifting and the like. There were some incidents at school: getting into fights, picking on some of the other kids, the usual things you'd expect at his age. He was smart. A good athlete and had a love for chemistry."

Artemis nodded. "And you said he was found last night?"

A hesitation, a quick exhale, but then Cynthia continued in the same clear, crisp tone. "Unfortunately, my husband was the one who answered the phone. I was sitting across the room, and I saw the moment when he heard. He dropped the phone, and he collapsed. He nearly toppled a chair." She swallowed again. Continued, "I raced over and picked up the phone. I remember it was nearly midnight, and we wouldn't normally have been awake that late, but we were helping one of our other favorite chess players prepare for the new blitz tournament. Which, by the way, congratulations for the invitation."

Cynthia added a quick, encouraging smile. But then she continued, "He was found hanging in this historic house that I mentioned on the phone. It's near where we live behind an old church in an empty, vacant lot maintained by the municipality."

Artemis knew this next part was the most delicate portion. She said, as carefully as she could, "And this girl he was with. She was found shot?"

Cynthia's eyelashes fluttered, and her hands gripped the steering wheel. She swallowed slowly but answered, "That's what the police said. They said Henry shot her, then hanged himself. The weapon was found at his feet, *they* said. They asked us to identify him, as his mother simply couldn't bring herself to."

"And did you?"

Cynthia nodded once. She was staring through the windshield, her hands perfectly manicured and gripping the steering wheel as if her life depended on it. "Yes, this morning. I didn't want to. And I made Henry stay at home. Not that I'm sure he would've been able to pull himself out of the room anyway. Like I told you, he was very close with our grandson. Almost... almost like a father figure."

Artemis could feel a tightening in her chest. She refused to give in to the emotional input, though.

"So the police found your grandson, hanging, with a gun at his feet?"

"Yes."

"And his girlfriend's body," Artemis said delicately, "I don't mean to upset you, but she was there too?"

"Dear, I'm already upset. You're not doing anything to add to it. I'm so grateful you've come..."

Mrs. Washington reached across the gap between them, patting Artemis' hand in a warm gesture. She returned her hand to the steering wheel, though, gripping it tightly again. "But yes, Henry's girlfriend, Paige, wasn't a very good influence on him. But he loved her. Was even going to marry her—at least, that's what he told his mother."

Artemis nodded slowly; she didn't say it out loud, but there was a chance Mrs. Washington was overestimating her grandson's course change over the last few years. Sometimes, teenagers just got better at hiding their choices.

"Alright, maybe it's best if I just see the place."

Cynthia nodded once more, her expression tight. She caught a sigh and a sob, and for a moment, she didn't seem to breathe at all.

Artemis exhaled for the both of them, turning to stare out the window and watch the passing terrain of Illinois. It was far flatter than Washington or California.

She wasn't sure what she had gotten herself into. She wouldn't be able to prove something if it wasn't true. From what she was hearing, the only alternative theory Cynthia had to go off was a grandmother's intuition.

Then again, in the past, Cynthia's intuition had been more than valuable in their late-night analysis sessions.

Artemis at least owed it to her to look into the horrible situation; another part of her, a smaller, cautious part, was worried she'd have to call in some favors.

It wasn't like she didn't have contacts. In fact, Agent Forester had even given her one of his business cards. Granted, it was for the boxing gym that he had an ownership stake in. But still, Forester was effective at his job.

Artemis still had three more days before she had to provide Agent Grant an answer on her offer to train out of the Seattle field office.

Artemis had spent years trying to avoid returning to the Pacific Northwest; she had avoided Pinelake. She didn't want to rehash old wounds. Most of the people in that town knew her only as the Ghostkiller's daughter who had once been a chess prodigy.

Artemis swallowed slowly, returning her attention to her clasped hands in her lap.

She could feel her nerves tingling. Her fingers felt strangely chilly.

Perhaps it was best she didn't involve anyone else.

Besides, even if she did call, there was no guarantee they would answer or even help. In addition, it might only be seen as a prelude to accepting Agent Grant's offer. And Artemis still wasn't sure she wanted to potentially work as a longer-term consultant.

On the other hand, there was information the FBI had that Artemis sorely needed. Information surrounding the disappearance of Artemis' sister nearly seventeen years ago.

Helen had disappeared. The first of her father's victims. At least, that's what Artemis had thought. But now she wasn't so sure. Was her father getting to her? Were his mind games working?

Or was there a chance, however small, that Helen was still alive?

A fighting chance.

The same sort of chance that Cynthia's grandson had of being innocent.

He was still dead, though. Would it matter to find out what had really happened?

Appearances, though, could be deceiving.

Artemis looked up again, feeling another, stronger surge of certainty that she would see this through. Not just for the sake of her friend. Though, that mattered. But also to prove to herself that sometimes, though rare, things weren't always what they seemed.

3

The door clicked shut behind Artemis, and she glanced back into the car through the half-open window. "Stay safe," she murmured quietly. "And stay here."

Mrs. Washington frowned out into the night. "Are you sure you don't want me to come with you?"

Artemis considered the offer. In part, she very *much* wanted someone to accompany her along the dark, unfamiliar suburban streets. On the other hand, Cynthia had said it was a safe neighborhood, and two figures were more likely to be spotted than one.

They'd already trundled down the road outside the historic home and then parked a block away due to the police car outside the crime scene.

Artemis swallowed, feeling a prickle along her skin. She forced a reassuring smile towards Cynthia then turned, jamming her hands in her pockets and moving down the sidewalk with slow, rolling steps. The lights behind her dimmed, and her shadow—cast before her—suddenly vanished.

She moved down the block and then turned along the street lined with hedges and carrying a lingering scent of the river passing by.

She could glimpse the water between the houses. It was late now, but the sky was clear, and the moon reflected off the water, tinging the windows of the parked cars lining the street.

Ahead, she spotted the police sedan.

It sat under a tree with long branches laden with rustling leaves. She hadn't spotted anyone *in* the vehicle when they'd driven slowly past, nor had she seen movement up the hill. But the last thing she needed was to get herself arrested outside Chicago.

"I should be studying," she muttered to herself, thinking of the chance to play the world champion in the upcoming blitz tournament. She'd spent years learning her craft. So what was she doing out at night, lurking in the dark?

She shook her head, trying to keep her mind on track. She approached the black gate circling the double lot behind a large, rectangular building that Mrs. Washington had said was a church. Artemis' most profound experience in a religious building was when her father had pretended to be a deacon in order to raise funds for a small orphanage in Morocco.

Of course... he'd spent all the money on a new car.

She shook her head, scowling at how many of her memories were soured by the ones of her father. The trees rustled above her, leaning over the black fence as if peeking across the sidewalk and down the street. Bright lights flashed at the intersection as a car turned, moving in the opposite direction.

She watched the vehicle leave, breathing slowly and feeling some relief it wasn't headed towards her.

She reached the black fence, pausing. The gate was taller than the fence. What were the chances someone had left it unlocked?

She frowned at the gate... and spotted the padlocked chain.

Shit.

She gritted her teeth and sighed, shaking her head in frustration and turning back towards the metal fence. Nothing for it.

She'd never been the most athletic person.

That had been Tommy. In her experience, he preferred scaling things as opposed to using doors. She reached out, her hand gripping the cold metal.

Artemis tried to vault the barricade, but really, it took three separate motions, the first two nearly ending with her impaling herself on the metal ornamentation topping the black fence.

With a grunt, flustered, and breathing heavily, Artemis dropped into the lawn. She rubbed her hands together, feeling a slow trickle along her palms.

A few stray leaves crunched underfoot, and the grass softened her footsteps. The house was strange, three stories tall, with distinct sections of brickwork and stucco.

She shot another look over her shoulder towards the parked police car. But there was no motion, no movement.

She reached up, slowly brushing her hair to the side.

"I hope they find my body," she muttered to herself, shaking her head.

As she moved across the ground, she felt a prickle along her spine.

The strange, pins and needles sensation moved along her back, and she picked up the pace as quietly as she could while angling towards the older, wooden stairs.

This had seemed like a better idea over the phone.

What exactly did she expect to discover?

The police had already been through.

They had ruled it a murder-suicide.

Normally, when investigating a crime scene in the past, she'd been accompanied by an FBI agent with a gun. Now, she didn't even have a set of keys sharp enough to protect herself.

She didn't have backup nor the ability to rely on an armed partner.

She forced a slow inhale and exhale, trying to breathe in the way one of her many counselors had taught her—the problem with most counselors, psychiatrists, and the like, was that they wanted to be the smartest person in the room...

Artemis reached the staircase.

A fluttering, yellow strip of caution tape barred the steps.

She paused, a finger lingering on the plastic. She was already trespassing—crossing into a crime scene, even on behalf of a friend, was the sort of thing her brother would do.

Her twin had spent a good amount of his time in and out of jail.

She sighed. She'd given her word.

She ducked under the caution tape and moved up the stairs.

The wooden boards creaked beneath her feet.

The chill wind settled across her shoulders, dabbing at her face.

The scent of old wood lingered heavily now. Her stomach tightened, but she exhaled slowly. The last place she wanted to have a panic attack was at a crime scene. She stooped, fingers moving towards a windowsill. Then, thinking better of touching it, she ducked lower.

A faint trail of dust ran along the windowsill. The only problem with this, though, was the wind.

She shot a look over her shoulder. Without the obstruction of too many trees or homes between the house and the river, the wind came quickly, in deep gusts.

She could feel it now, ruffling her hair and sweeping across her form.

The rest of the wooden surfaces, on the floor and along the edge of the house, only had a thin layer of dust. But here, on the windows, there were a couple of patches where it had clumped.

She glanced at her own feet, lifting one to examine the bottom of her shoe; a couple of pine leaves stuck in the rubber grooves with patches of mud from where she had jumped over the fence. The ground had felt soft at the base of the hill... had someone climbed *through* the window?

But she knew better than to settle on first assumptions. Oftentimes, it was best to take different ideas, synthesize them, and see the result.

Most chess players could think a few moves ahead; most professional chess players could think as many as ten or more moves ahead, calculating every eventuality.

Those ten moves were not linear but, rather, parts of a long branching string of possibilities. She bit the corner of her lip, focusing.

Muddy feet on the windowsill. Option one. Perhaps the police officer had scraped his foot off. But no, the mud was too far back. Maybe a gardener had rested a trowel there. She ran through a few more potential options, considering.

But then, refocusing, she decided the most likely explanation was her first one.

Inexperienced chess players often tried to win early. But professionals knew the best path to victory was to seize small victories over time. Oftentimes, it wasn't even by taking pieces. At the highest level, most games were played with even material. But it was about position. It was about anticipating something ten moves ahead. Seizing the center of a board, making sure all of her developed bishops and knights had material protecting them. Keeping her pawn structures strong. Isolating opponent structures. Castling before it was too late. Not bringing the queen out too early.

There were many basics. Things that most players knew but didn't realize the importance of.

She had once played an entire game, fifty moves, where back and forth she had grappled with her opponent for the rook files; in the end, she had won by seizing a single open rank on the edge of the board.

And so, with an eye for the inconsequential, she glanced around again, her gaze trailing over the ground, moving from the windowsill to the door.

Then, carefully, using her hem to protect her fingers, she pushed open the door.

The hinges groaned with age. The floorboards creaked in protest.

She let out a shaking breath.

As her eyes adjusted to the dark interior of the old, historic home, she felt a slow chill...

A noose was still dangling from the curling banister. There was still a stain of blood, most of it cleaned, painting the ground beneath the stairs.

Her eyes darted around in the dark, but now she could barely see. In order to gather information, she would need more light.

And so, carefully, she withdrew her phone, glanced over her shoulder and then, wishing she didn't have to, but feeling it was the only way to keep herself from being spotted, she hooked the door with her heel and closed it slowly, sealing herself inside the house.

As the door shut and her flashlight *clicked* on from her phone, she projected the beam of light towards the noose.

She glared at the thing, shivering.

It had been roped to the banister; she looked down towards the bloodstain on the ground.

For a moment, she felt queasy. She couldn't imagine what Cynthia Washington was going through.

Part of Artemis' own story was that she didn't know what had happened to her sister—didn't know if Helen was dead or not. Certainty, she felt, was more earth shattering, but uncertainty was harder to heal from.

She shook her head and glanced along the ground.

One thing she did notice. A small wooden bench against the wall—high enough that Henry could have used it.

But as she approached, she noted some cobwebs extending from the wooden legs to the wall.

Mostly undisturbed.

The bench hadn't been moved.

Which meant, she thought as she retraced her steps, glancing at the stairs, that however Henry had died, he had jumped or been pushed over the banister after the rope had been wrapped around his neck. Unless there was another furniture piece the police had moved...

She considered this and glanced towards the stairs.

There was an old, rickety chair which had been pushed aside into an adjacent room. But by the way it was positioned, right in the threshold, she decided it wasn't in a natural position.

She approached the chair, studying a thin trail of blood along the front of the backrest—she hesitated, frowning.

"Now, that doesn't make sense," she said softly. She glanced over her shoulder again, then back at the chair. She sidestepped it and raised her flashlight, illuminating the back.

No blood.

Only blood on the front.

And then she heard the sound of groaning hinges.

She spun around, going suddenly still. The door to the house opened wide. Two bright flashlights glared at her like demonic eyes in the dark.

They spotlighted her, casting her silhouette over her shoulder, across the ground.

"Hands up!" a deep voice shouted. "Put your hands where we can see them!"

With a yelp, she dropped her phone and instantly complied. "I'm with the FBI," she yelled.

The moment she said it, she regretted it. But it was the first thing that came to mind.

The two flashlights lowered slowly. "You have ID?" one of them barked.

Vaguely, she glimpsed the blue uniforms of police officers. Even the way they raised and lowered their lights had an air of authority about it.

She wasn't sure how Tommy so often faced people like this without collapsing.

Now, her voice was shaking. "I'm a consultant."

She heard the sound of rattling metal handcuffs. One of the officers was moving towards her now. "Turn around," he said firmly, "Hands behind your back!"

Artemis winced but didn't object. She turned slowly, releasing a pent-up breath.

4

Artemis fidgeted uncomfortably in the interrogation room. This was not the first time.

In recent weeks, she'd been on the *other* side of the table. But befo re... as a teenager? She could remember the haranguing, the intrusive questions. When her father had been arrested, they'd demanded to know why Artemis hadn't *done* anything.

Of course, she'd never known. Not until after.

Now, sitting there in the cold, metal chair, she could feel her mind darting back to those unpleasant memories. Her wrists shifted in the handcuffs, feeling the bite of the metal loops against her skin. She winced and shifted again with a scraping sound where the chain dragged across the table.

She shot a look towards the door's thick, steel frame. Above, the blinking red light glared at her from a security camera.

She had spent a few hours in a holding cell. Now, this would be the second round of interrogation.

So far, she hadn't had a panic attack.

She was inhaling for five seconds, exhaling for seven.

It's a battle of the mind. Another small piece of advice from Helen. Though her sister was five years older, Helen had been Artemis' best friend before she'd vanished.

Suddenly, the door opened.

It moved seamlessly on perfectly oiled hinges. Without a sound. The footsteps, though, tapped staccato against the cold floor.

Two figures entered. First, a man with a shaved head and thick rimmed glasses perched on a flat nose; he looked more like a librarian than a police officer. He had a small, white goatee and wore neat slacks and a matching jacket, with a small stencil of a red rose over his lapel. Despite the late hour, he looked alert and awake.

The second figure was a young woman, perhaps no older than twenty-five. She had her hair tied back in a bun and wore two simple, silver earrings. She was yawning as she entered and carried a folder in one hand and her phone in the other.

The two of them sat down at the chairs across the table without saying a word. The door slowly swung shut, the red light of the camera still blinking.

"Good to meet you, Ms. Blythe," the man with the shaved head and goatee said. He adjusted the glasses, studying her peculiarly. As he moved his frames, they magnified his eyes before settling back to a more appropriate proportion.

She glanced between the two of them.

"You're the detectives on the case?"

"Very astute," said the man. "I'm Detective Ross. This is Detective Hardwick."

Artemis glanced at the younger woman, who had placed the folder on the table. She was now laying glossy photos on the surface between them.

Instantly, after a risky glance, Artemis knew she did not want to study those photos too closely.

"We hear you claim to work with the FBI," said Detective Ross. "Impersonating a federal officer is a serious offense."

He had crossed his legs, displaying a crimson sock just beneath the perfectly pressed hem of his trousers. He spoke in an off-putting, accommodating sort of way but Artemis frowned at his tone.

It was congenial, almost friendly, but she knew the voice was a trick. The calm demeanor a trap. As she glanced between the two of them, her eyes taking in what information she could, she felt a little shiver of fear.

She said, "You're joking."

"No, I'm not. The offense is very—"

"No, not that. You think I had something to do with the murder?" She shook her head, bewildered. She studied the man, her eyes moving along his hands glancing at his fingernails. The first flaw she spotted were the nails on the second and third finger. He chewed his nails. The woman leaned forward, listening to the exchange between the older man and Artemis. She had a serious expression and inclined her chair a bit *too* far to the right, away from the other detective.

Artemis cataloged all of this in a split second.

"A strange question," said Detective Ross. "Do you mind if I ask what makes you think we suspect you?"

"You're leading with a strong arm," Artemis said quickly. "Which means you know who I am. Which means you know who my father is. And because you didn't mention it first but, rather, are allowing me to introduce myself, you're fishing. Besides, it's very late. They wouldn't bring two detectives in to deal with a trespasser."

Artemis frowned, staring across the table and feeling the knot in her chest tighten.

Detective Ross adjusted his glasses again then rested his hands flat on the table. "Very curious. And you reached that conclusion just based on our brief exchange? Nothing else you want to add, perhaps?"

Artemis nodded once. She could feel her stomach twisting. The anxiety rising.

Her father's reputation was following her even in Chicago; hundreds of miles away she was still the Ghostkiller's daughter.

Now the younger detective leaned in, frowning. "It's a good bluff," she said, her tone equal parts sarcasm and irritation. She yawned again but held a hand over her mouth and continued a second later, "But you know what I think is a better explanation for your little intuition?"

Artemis didn't say anything but preferred to study the woman.

"Maybe you're involved," she said. "And so you know we suspect you. So why don't we skip this charming, little game of yours and get straight to the point. Why were you at the crime scene?"

Artemis wrinkled her nose. "I study people. It isn't a game."

Detective Hardwick seemed to be struggling to resist the urge to roll her eyes. She glanced at Detective Ross, cleared her throat, then said, "You were lying about the FBI. Now you're playing games. Why not tell us what you were really up to?" She frowned at Artemis.

Artemis bit her lip, inhaling, exhaling, trying to keep herself in check. She knew it was best she didn't antagonize these two—especially not Hardwick. The young woman was sitting forward and a bit overzealous, clearly trying to make a statement.

Artemis didn't want to be the punctuation.

"I *did* work with the FBI in Seattle," Artemis said quietly. "I gave you Agent Forester's card, didn't I?"

Hardwick shook her head stubbornly. "Just because you read the name of an agent from an article in your hometown," she said, savoring the information as if she too had just made a deduction, "Doesn't mean that you work for them."

Artemis, feeling her own irritability rising, replied, "They hired me to pay attention to the small details. Like I was doing at the crime scene."

Detective Ross looked curious; Hardwick just rolled her eyes.

"Did you find anything useful?" said Hardwick in a tone that hinted she already knew the answer was no.

Artemis didn't yell, didn't insult. But she sat a bit straighter and then, clearly and concisely, said, "A thing or two, yes. I know you don't believe, but you should. For instance, if I wasn't good at noticing details, how would I know you two are sleeping together? And that currently internal issues are rising, and your boss is suspicious. And so recently, you," she said, pointing directly at Hardwick, "have requested a bit of a break. And you," she said, looking at Detective Ross, "pretend like you're okay with it, but you find the whole business irritating."

The moment she finished, Artemis slouched a bit, her handcuffs shifting against the table. *One enemy at a time.* Another piece of guidance she tried to live by. And now she was picking fights with the people investigating her.

How late *was* it?

Detective Ross blinked in surprise, but Hardwick shot a horrified look towards the camera over the door then back again. She stood up angrily. "How dare you?"

"If I was wrong," Artemis said, wearily, "you would have treated it as just another one of my little lies."

Of course, it was far more than a guess. First of all, the way Hardwick had been leaning away from the other agent was just a bit too much. As if to compensate for something. When they had *entered* the room, they had been standing close, with no discomfort, but when they had moved into view of the camera, which was still recording, Hardwick had used her physical language to tell the camera and whoever was watching that there was nothing between her and detective Ross. It was the subtleties of body language that mattered most. Leaning too far away.

The way Detective Ross hadn't looked angry but, rather, hurt by the distance suggested there was affection involved. Their age difference and the nature of their work relationship implied that the concern was more bureaucratic than personal.

The fact that it was the camera that Detective Hardwick was most concerned about also implied the feelings weren't gone, but the appearance of them had to be. Which implied recent developments. And usually detectives were at the top chain in a police station. The only concern would have been if someone higher up started to ask questions about the nature of their relationship.

Of course, for Artemis, all of this had been processed in a matter of seconds. It was the benefit of studying human emotion, body language, details.

It had still been a guess but an educated guess, stated confidently. In her father's old job as a mentalist, that was key. Confidence.

But more than confidence, stating something confidently in order to gauge reaction. Oftentimes, the first thing a mentalist said didn't have to be true. It was the *reaction* to that thing which actually provided further information.

There were a number of alternative options that could have resulted from her spark of question and accusation. But now, with Hardwick on her feet, feigning outrage that hadn't been present before, Artemis felt at least eighty percent confident that most of what she had said was true.

Detective Ross shook his head. "I assure you," he said in a clear but polite voice, "My partner and I are purely platonic," he said, folding his hands. "Do you enjoy issuing wild accusations?"

Artemis didn't reply. Hardwick was slowly lowering back into her chair, clearly perturbed by the comments. She was glaring but also shot more than one glance towards the door, despite herself.

Artemis was now eighty-five percent convinced she was right. Not that it mattered. Irritating these two wasn't helpful. So, instead, she leaned back again and exhaled slowly. "I'm telling you the truth. I really do work with the FBI. Did you call Agent Forester? That business card I gave the arresting officer..."

Detective Ross nodded once, seemingly eager to move onto a new subject. "We placed a call a few hours ago, but that number was for a business owner at a gym."

"Did he say he was the FBI?"

Detective Hardwick snapped, "He said he was a professional stripper and wanted to know if we were looking to hire."

Artemis hesitated, staring, wondering if the woman was joking.

But neither detective was smiling.

Artemis let out a faint, little breath. Perhaps it had been the wrong number, but more likely, that had been Forester's version of a joke.

Exhaustion weighed heavy. Artemis felt her mind starting to get foggy.

She shifted uncomfortably at the table and raised a foot to shake it, where it had gone numb.

Detective Ross pressed the glossy photos, sliding them towards Artemis. "Why don't you tell us what you make of these?"

Artemis glanced down, frowning at the photographs.

She had wanted to avoid looking at them entirely.

But, she realized, there might not be another chance to get a glance at crime scene photos.

The photographs revealed an illuminated version of the historic home's atrium. The noose was there but so was the body of a young man and there, on the ground beneath him, a young woman in a pool of blood.

Even staring at the photographs, Artemis could feel her heart pounding.

She spotted the gun laying on the ground near the bench she had seen.

She tried not to study the faces of the victims. She wasn't sure if this would make it any easier, but she simply couldn't bring herself to stare.

She spotted the chair which had been toppled beneath the hanging youth.

And that was when she hesitated.

The chair was lying on its back next to the puddle of blood.

"The chair," Artemis said, slowly. "Did someone move it?"

"We moved it," snapped Hardwick. She was still glaring daggers at Artemis. "We had to get it out of the way for forensics. Now what do *you* know about the chair?"

Instead of answering, Artemis said, slowly, "And who found it?"

But Hardwick shook her head furiously. "We're asking the questions. So what's your grand deduction?"

Artemis studied the photo. To her, it was glaringly obvious. And as she stared, she felt a slow lump form in her throat. Just to be sure, though, she said, quietly, "Did anyone do anything to the chair?"

The detectives glanced at each other then back at her. Detective Ross said, "We moved it, that was all. Are you saying you *do* know something about the crime scene?"

Artemis held her tongue. The more she told them, the more likely they were to assume she had been involved.

Her job wasn't to show off. It was to figure out a way to get them to believe her.

So she lied. "I can't see anything that stands out."

She grimaced as she glanced at the photographs again and realized her hands were shaking. She clasped them together, trying to keep them still.

Detective Ross said, "We saw a bit of the transcript of the previous interview you had with the police."

Artemis frowned. "You mean when I was a teenager?"

Hardwick said, "Your father had a big influence on you, didn't he? He was a liar too. That's how he made his living, wasn't it?"

Artemis noticed the intentional use of the word *too*. She didn't comment on it, though. Instead, she glanced once more at the crime scene photos, making sure she wasn't mistaken. But no, the clue was staring right at her. Which made things worse. Because if she told the police, they would think the only reason she knew was because she had been there at the time of the murders. But if she didn't tell them, it meant that they would be missing a key piece of the puzzle.

It was as this horrible thought swirled through her mind, that she heard a playful knock on the door.

Three quick retorts, followed by a rolling tap-*tap-tap*.

The detectives frowned, glancing at the door.

Artemis looked over as well. And then, there was a *click*, and the door was pushed open.

A voice in the hall was saying, "Not yet, agent. Please, just wait—"

But a familiar voice cut off the objection with, "Don't worry, I play a professional on TV."

And then, a tall man with unkempt, brown hair, and a lumpy left ear marched into the interrogation room, grinning as if he had just been given a surprise party.

"Hey, Checkers," he said with a cheerful wave.

She stared at him.

Forester glanced at the two detectives across the table. He gave another cheeky wave, winking at each of them.

Hardwick was scowling now. Forester said, "I see you've been making friends." He glanced at Artemis again, raising his eyebrows.

She stared back at him. "What are you doing here?"

Detective Ross was rising to his feet, frowning for the first time since he had entered the room. "I'd like to ask the same question. Who are you?"

"You can call me Cameron. I'm the stripper for hire you ordered." He nodded solemnly. "But sometimes, I also pretend to be an FBI agent, like Checkers here. Now, as for what I'm doing here," he said, hands in his pocket now. "I'm here to get you out, Ms. Blythe. Or is that not why you asked them to call me?"

Artemis wasn't even sure how to respond. In part, she felt a weird sense of relief. In the strange, hostile police station, sitting in cuffs, having spent hours being held or interrogated, it was good to have some backup. On the other hand, she wished the backup would wipe that shit-eating grin off his face.

There was something jovial, lighthearted, about the sociopath's attitude. She noticed he also still hadn't figured out how to properly button his suit. A few of the buttons were in the wrong slots. As she took in his appearance, giving a quick once over, she noticed he was still wearing wrinkled pants. At least, this time his socks matched. Then again, the shoes didn't. One was a sleek, black dress shoe. The other was a sneaker.

Agent Cameron Forester tugged at his left, lumpy ear, a gift from his fighting days when he had competed as a professional mixed martial artist. He had once described himself as a friend to the gangsters, criminals, and lowlifes of the world.

His aunt, Agent Shauna Grant, was in charge of the field office where Forester worked. But the last time Artemis had checked, this office had been in Seattle, not Illinois.

Forester began to move in Artemis' direction, wiggling a key between his fingers. "Got this from the desk," he said. "I don't mind if I do." He bent over, extending the key towards the lock.

Detective Ross shot a look towards the door, but it had swung closed again.

Hardwick didn't seem to have a particularly wide range of emotions and was still scowling. She leaned forward to quickly gather the crime scene photos so Forester couldn't see them.

"Do you mind showing us some identification?" Ross said, quietly. He was no longer frowning and had resumed his air of calm.

"Are we talking for my nighttime ventures or federal?"

Ross gave a polite smile to humor the agent. Hardwick was now standing as well. Agent Forester shrugged. "Tough audience." He pulled out his badge, raising it and showing it to the two detectives.

Forester said, in a bit more serious of a tone, "Your boss sent me back here with the full support of your department. Something about wanting to work together with the federals. Though, my guess is he doesn't want us trying to poach this case. Low closure rate, I'm guessing, huh? Too bad."

Forester beamed and then unhooked the handcuffs. Artemis felt another surge of relief; she managed to lift her hands, massaging her wrists.

Forester glanced between the two detectives. "Well, if that's all, I really should be taking Checkers here."

Artemis noticed the edge of a tattoo peaking past Forester's collar.

His unprofessional appearance and doubly unprofessional behavior only further seemed to irritate Hardwick, who was leaning in and whispering fiercely in her partner's ear.

But Detective Ross held up a single finger. "Would you mind waiting here for just a few minutes while I clear this up?"

Again, polite, clear, but also, Artemis wondered how he would act if they refused.

Still, Forester didn't seem to care. He said, "Sure. Just got off a flight, don't mind me if I don't sit."

He moved to the edge of the room and leaned against the wall, crossing his arms and reclining.

Detective Ross nodded politely, then, with a quick tug on the arm of his partner, he led her back out the door.

Once more it opened with a *click* and swung silently shut.

5

Artemis continued to rub at her wrists, frowning towards where Forester leaned casually back against a glass window, his long legs angling out, his arms crossed. She glimpsed a white scar trailing along the man's wrist, across his palm as he opened and closed his hand.

"Well," said Forester.

"Why are you here?" she said. "Did you fly in?"

He nodded once. "Had a case in Florida—layover in Indiana." He shrugged. "Only a half hour flight. How's it going? You're looking better than the last time I saw you."

She frowned. "The last time you saw me, I had a dead giant bleeding on me."

"Hmm. Fair. But actually, I was there at the hospital too."

Artemis let out a little sigh. The problem with Agent Forester was determining how seriously to take him. He was a dangerous man, that much was clear. But he also treated the world a bit like a schoolboy would. She remembered once, two cases ago, when he'd rolled the car window down to ask for directions from a couple of drug dealers.

Forester was a self-proclaimed sociopath. He had anti-social personality disorder, which meant he couldn't form connections the same
way most people did. To her surprise, when she'd looked up the condi-
tion, there were a good number of citizens who lived perfectly normal,
comfortable lives. Not every sociopath turned out to be a killer like her
father.

But also, Forester came with a strange disinterest for danger—as if
he simply couldn't sense fear.

Now, she swallowed slowly, studying the man. She pushed to her
feet, still rubbing at her wrists and shooting a glance towards the
camera over the door.

"Thanks... thanks for coming," she said cautiously.

Forester nodded once, tapping two heavily calloused fingers to his
forehead in something of a mock salute. "My pleasure," he said. "Want
to know why I'm here?"

Artemis sighed. "Please don't say—"

"To help."

"Oh... Okay. I thought you were going to say..." She frowned, trailing off, then shook her head and sighed.

Forester sniffed once, running a hand through his hair, clearly dis-
interested. "But nah, I'm *sort* of joking. You helped us out on the last
two." He winked. "Plus, Agent Grant asked me to do right by you."
He nodded as if impressed. "She must *really* see something in you to
tell me to reroute."

Artemis considered this comment. Agent Grant had pitched
Artemis on training with the FBI. As for Forester, there was a lot she
didn't know. Thinking of him as anyone's kin was odd. But also, she
remembered the way her father had toyed with the agent the last time
they'd visited the prison where he was incarcerated. Her father had
hinted at knowledge about Forester's past.

Specifically, something that had happened seven years ago.

Whatever her father knew—*however* he knew it—the information seemed to rankle Forester. This was a strange man. A dangerous man, but a competent agent. And for the moment, in that precinct, the only friend she had.

"They're ruling the case a murder-suicide," she said cautiously, feeling a bit more at ease now that she knew someone in the room.

"I see. That's why you were caught snooping around the place?"

Artemis nodded once. "I was trying to help a friend. Her grandson was one of the victims."

"One of?" His eyebrows went higher. "So you're thinking our two lovebird detectives got it wrong?"

Artemis threw up her hands in a show of emotion. "Thank you!" she declared. "So you saw it, too?"

"Oh, hell yeah. Those two are doing the dirty dozen."

"I—I don't know what that means. No, wait, please—don't explain it." Artemis lowered her hand from where she'd upheld a finger. She said, carefully, "But did you see the crime scene photos?"

"Just got a glance as the blonde cutie snatched them up."

"I—oh... Forester..." Artemis huffed, closing her eyes for a moment. It wasn't her job to teach every sociopath basic etiquette. She endeavored to stay on track. "Well, I was at the house."

"Trespassing."

"Right, yes. And I saw the chair in the photos."

Forester was frowning now, his expression a bit more serious as he studied her. "Shit," he said. "What's that look, Blythe? You saying this *wasn't* a murder-suicide?"

"No, it wasn't," she said firmly. "It was a double murder. The chair," she insisted, "in the photos, is on its back."

"And?"

"And," she said, clearly, lowering her voice and looking away from the camera, "the blood was on the *front* cushion of the backrest. None on the *back* of the chair."

Forester hesitated, and then he let out a sudden breath. "Wait... so the chair fell *first*. And then the blood spilled."

She nodded, pointing at him. "Exactly. If I poured paint on the ground, then put a book on the paint, the entire cover would be stained. But if I put the *book* down first. And then poured paint around it, there would be no paint on the front. At least, not much. Which means, the chair was on the ground *first*. After Henry was hanged. *Then* Paige was shot. The blood came second. Henry couldn't have shot her."

"Wait," he said... "You're sure?"

"Very."

The door opened again and Artemis and Forester both glanced over. Detective Ross stood in the doorway. There was no sign of his partner. He said, "I'm afraid I don't understand. Pardon, but I didn't catch that last part."

Artemis hesitated, frowning at the thought that the man had simply been lingering outside the door.

"We check out, boss?" said Forester.

Ross nodded primly at the poorly dressed agent. "Yes. Much appreciation for your patience." He looked back at Artemis. "But as to what you were saying..."

She let out a faint exhale. Then, deciding that with Forester in the room, she was safe enough from incrimination, she said, "The chair was on the ground, right?"

"Yes."

"On its back."

"I... yes, I'm looking at the photo now." His phone was in his hand, and he was frowning at it.

"Well, go back and look at the chair. No one did anything to it, according to your partner. There was *no* blood on the back of the chair. Which means the chair was on the ground *before* the blood."

Artemis waited excitedly. But Detective Ross was just smiling quizzically at her.

She swallowed, trying again.

"Sir, if Henry Rodine killed his girlfriend and *then* stepped onto a chair, adjusted the noose, and only *then* hanged himself, the blood would *already* be on the ground. He would kick the chair over, where it landed with the back to the floor, and the blood would have soaked the *back* of the chair. See?"

Ross was frowning now.

"Because there's no blood on the back of the chair," Forester said simply, nodding, "It means he was hanged *first*. Then she was shot."

"Exactly!" Artemis declared. "And how does a man who's been hanged shoot someone?"

"Well..." Ross hesitated, lowering his phone. "Perhaps he shot her *as* he hanged himself."

Artemis frowned skeptically. "You think he climbed onto a chair, gun in his hand, aimed it, tied a noose around his neck and his girlfriend didn't run? Didn't do anything? Just stood there, knowing exactly what was coming? You think before killing her, he would put himself in a vulnerable position? That's not how humans work, sir."

"Well, what if he shot her as he fell?"

"Same issue," Artemis replied. "Plus look where the gun landed. Directly beneath him. If he was raising an arm or lowering it to fire the gun and then he hanged himself, kicking out a chair, the momentum would have sent the gun *forward* not straight down."

"This is... speculation," Ross said carefully.

Artemis tried to hide her exasperation. Speculation didn't mean inaccurate. Especially speculation with likelihoods and probabilities. It made sense to her. Human nature was a matter of percentages, not certainties.

But she said, carefully. "Sir, which is *more* likely. That she was shot, then he was hanged. Or that he noosed himself, climbed on a chair, kicked the chair, and only *then* fired a shot at a girl, who wasn't restrained, had no bindings but just stood there, watching him. And then, on top of it, the gun fell *straight* down."

"We found gunpowder residue on his hands," Ross insisted.

"Which hand?"

"Both," Ross said.

"But... but that doesn't make sense!"

"It does," Forester said, "especially if he was holding the weapon with both hands."

Ross nodded.

"But see!" Artemis exclaimed. "Now we think he was also *holding the gun with two hands,* while standing on a chair with a noose around his neck, and his girlfriend doing *nothing* to run, to duck, to hide? It's not probable."

"The evidence is clear," said Ross firmly. "Gunpowder on both hands. A history of crime."

Artemis snorted. "Shoplifting and petty theft."

Here, though, Ross shook his head. "No, in fact. Not just shop-lifting and petty theft. Mr. Rodine put a young man in the hospital. Damaged the boy's eye so badly, he'll never see out of it again."

Artemis hesitated. "Wait... really?"

"Really," Ross replied, tone cold.

Artemis frowned. Mrs. Washington hadn't told her this part. Perhaps the boy's grandmother didn't even know.

Artemis hesitated. "This boy he injured—is he still local?"

"Yes," Ross said. "But I believe that is besides the point. You are free to go, Ms. Blythe," Detective Ross said, extending an arm towards the metal door.

Artemis glanced past him, frowning and shaking her head. "You're making a mistake. This wasn't a murder-suicide."

He didn't react, keeping his arm extended, frowning at her now.

Artemis shifted uncomfortably. She didn't want to leave. Not now. Not yet. Not while she was so close.

"Please," she said, insistently. "Is this because of what I said about you and your partner? I'm sorry. But—"

"What you said about Detective Hardwick and me," he retorted, cutting her off, "was nothing other than bold-faced fabrication. You'll forgive me if I don't suddenly develop a streak of trust for you. You've been lying, trespassing, and it's time for you to leave."

He reached out, grabbed the door handle, and opened it for her.

Artemis sighed. She wanted to protest more, but Agent Forester reached her side, extended an arm, placed a hand in the small of her back, and began to gently push her towards the door.

"But, but—"

"Later," Forester muttered. "Let it go."

She felt a surge of frustration. The reputation of a young man was on the line. Cynthia's husband was bedridden, hiding from the world because of his grief.

The family would never be the same if she didn't clear Henry's name. But how was she supposed to do that if the police were ignoring her?

Still, she allowed Forester to guide her out of the interrogation room.

He led her down a bleak hall illuminated by a single stretch of tube lights.

The two of them approached sliding doors past a row of protective glass counters.

Forester approached the sliding doors first, giving a little wave towards where an officer behind a desk was typing at her computer.

And then Forester led her out onto marble steps, towards the gray parking lot. As they moved away from the precinct, out into the fresh air, Forester pulled his phone from his pocket, frowning as he marched forward.

"Who are you calling?"

"Wade."

"Why?"

He shot her a look, coming to a stop next to a sedan with tinted windows. "Because I was supposed to be back in Seattle about two hours ago. Agent Wade is waiting at the airport."

She winced. "He hasn't been waiting long, has he?"

Forester waved a dismissive hand. "Couple hours isn't much."

Artemis winced.

Forester lowered his phone after a few moments, frowning. "Too late. He's not picking up."

Artemis said slowly, "Thank you for..." she trailed off and shrugged. "Thank you."

He glanced at her, nodded once. "Grant says you're thinking of joining the team."

She sighed, rubbing at the back of her head. "I wish she wouldn't tell that to people. I haven't made up my mind."

Forester crossed his arms. "It's because of me, isn't it?"

She stared at him.

He nodded. "You find me intimidating. Attractive. I don't blame you. But I give you my word, we can make it work."

He said it solemnly, eyes fixated on her.

She stammered, swallowed, and then he smirked, winking at her and turning towards the car.

She frowned at the back of Forester's shoulders. She had to remind herself, whatever he appeared to be, this was not a safe person. Her father had some sort of leverage over the agent. Had some information hanging over the man's head.

If ever there was someone her father could use or manipulate, it was a sociopath working for the federal government. She wasn't sure if Cameron was trying to be funny or rude. She wasn't sure if he even knew the difference; she released a faint sigh as the lights flashed.

"Here's your stuff by the way," Forester said, reaching into his pocket and pulling out a phone. He glanced at the digital clock on the device and gave a low whistle. "Shit—getting late. You got a hotel yet or want me to book one on Grant's card?"

"Umm... she won't mind?"

He shrugged, opening the door to the parked car and gesturing for her to enter. "What she doesn't know won't hurt her. Besides, she's the one who's talking big about getting you back to Seattle."

Artemis hesitated, wondering if she ought to call Mrs. Washington first or wait until morning... She sighed, shaking her head and then approached the vehicle, slipping into the car.

Whatever Detective Ross said, Artemis knew Henry Rodine was innocent. And so far, her list of suspects was slowly expanding. At first, she'd wondered if the girlfriend had been the one to pull the trigger on herself after forcing Henry to hang himself...

But the gun was too far away, and *two* gunshots to the chest ruled this theory out. But on the other hand... if Henry had injured someone and sent him to the hospital, then chances were that someone held a grudge.

Enough of a grudge to kill?

Artemis was going to have to do some digging.

6

Artemis pressed her phone against her cheek as she slipped the key card into the hotel door slot.

Back in her hometown, there was only one hotel to speak of. And it wasn't a particularly nice one. This hotel, however, had fresh carpeting; in addition, there were no giant serial killers hiding in her bedroom as she arrived.

This didn't stop her, though, from lingering outside in the hall and giving a quick once over, glancing around the room. The last time, the aforementioned giant had nearly killed her. But Forester had managed to shoot him through the drywall.

Once Artemis had determined the room was safe and the only real threat came in the form of suspect chocolate placed on her pillow, she relaxed and slipped into the room.

Her phone finally connected, the glass chill against her cheek. "Hello, *Artemis*?" It was Cynthia Washington, and her voice sounded on the verge of panic.

"Cynthia? Is everything okay?"

A quick, desperate exhalation. "Thank God, you're okay. What happened? I stayed for nearly three hours. Where are you?"

Artemis winced. She had assumed Cynthia had seen the police take her away.

"I'm sorry," Artemis said quickly. "I had a bit of a run in with the police."

A gasp. A hastily muttered prayer. "I am so sorry," Cynthia retorted. "Tell me where. I'm coming now. Can I post bail?"

Artemis shook her head but then stopped, wrinkling her nose and realizing no one could see her. "No, that's fine. Thank you. I'm out. I had another friend of mine help."

A bit of hesitation. Then, "I didn't know you had friends in the area."

Artemis said, "You know what, it's fine. I actually have a hotel. I think I'm going to stay in the area for a couple more days."

"Really? Did you, what was—" Mrs. Washington paused, and Artemis thought she heard a voice in the background. Then, Cynthia continued in a much quieter voice, "Sorry, Henry is trying to sleep." She breathed heavily then, steadying herself, she continued in a more clear, crisp tone, "All right. What can I do to help? Do you need anything?"

"I should be fine. Thank you."

For a moment, Artemis considered mentioning what she had seen. Mentioning the clue with the chair. Her near confidence that Henry had been a murder victim rather than the perpetrator.

But there was too much she didn't know. There was still a chance that Henry was behind this and had an accomplice. Or even that someone had spotted what he had done and then killed him in retaliation. There were too many unknown quantities.

And so, she simply said, "I'm fine for now. Thank you so much. One thing you could do for me. Did you..." Artemis trailed off, then said, quickly, like ripping a band-aid. "Did you know your grandson put someone in the hospital a couple of years ago?"

"Excuse me?"

Artemis winced. "I didn't think so. Very sorry. You don't happen to know who it was, do you?"

Some vague murmuring, a pause. Then, a hastily cleared throat. "Let me ask my daughter. I can get back to you first thing tomorrow morning."

Artemis said, "It's late. Take your time. Thank you."

They gave their farewells, and Artemis hung up; only then did she lower her phone and glance around the small hotel room. A single bed, twice as large as she was used to. There were bars on the window; this seemed odd as well but at least the grate was curled, painted white, and looked ornamental.

A small refrigerator slotted next to the bed, and one of the chocolates on the pillows looked as if it was melting.

She sighed, picking up the silver wrapper, delicately balancing the chocolate as she approached a sink near the fridge then tossed the wrapper into a basin.

As she did, she heard a sudden knock on her door.

Artemis hesitated. She felt a slow prickle along her spine, once again remembering her last interaction in a hotel room.

She swallowed faintly, double checking that she had her phone on her, just in case she needed to make a quick emergency call.

"Hello?" she said slowly.

"Artemis?" Forester's voice replied.

He sounded urgent.

"Is everything okay?"

"Open the door," Forester said, his voice terse. "I found something."

It was credit to just how much Forester discombobulated her, that she didn't know if she should be curious or terrified about the prospect of opening the door to her hotel room with Cameron on the other side.

She hesitated, then said, "What is it?"

"There was another double murder. Just like this. Four months ago," he said, his voice muffled through the door.

But Artemis was no longer hesitant. She hurried forward, swinging the door open and staring out.

Forester was no longer wearing his mis-buttoned suit jacket. But instead had a T-shirt with two boxing gloves printed on the chest.

He was frowning at his phone, scratching at his lumpy ear. "Look at this," he said.

She glanced at the phone, swallowing slowly.

The article headline read: *Murder-suicide shocks Warrenville!*

She went on to read the article, her eyes skipping along the paragraphs. As she read, she felt a cold dread fill her stomach.

"It's just like Henry," she murmured. "When was this again?"

Forester was tapping the top of the screen.

She spotted a date hidden just below the banner. "Four months. Only four months," she said slowly. "How far is Warrenville from here?"

She looked up. Forester shook his head. "Only about twenty minutes. Maybe half an hour on a bad day of traffic."

Artemis felt a slow tingle along her spine.

Forester was still scratching at his ear. "I'm no police detective," he said, "but that sure doesn't look like a coincidence to me. The chair found toppled in a pool of blood? Two teenagers, one of them hanged, the other shot?" He was shaking his head, frowning as he did.

Artemis swallowed faintly. "How long was the investigation?"

Forester shook his head. "Don't know. Honestly, I'm probably not supposed to tamper. Unless," he said, slowly. He looked at her then shrugged. "We could get the band back together?"

Artemis felt a pit in her stomach. "What do you mean?"

"Agent Wade waited at that airport for three hours. He clearly doesn't have anything better to do."

"He waited for *you*."

Cameron nodded and tapped his nose. "You make a good point. My aunt was mentioning that things were slow. I bet you I could get them to fly out here, take the case federal."

She stared. "You would do that?"

"My aunt would do it, for a consultant. There're perks to working for Agent Grant," he said with a knowing nod. "She's tough but deeply loyal. If you are on the team," he said, slowly, "there's a good chance she'd fly out here with Wade and help us out. She might not come herself, but she'd at least give me permission to use some of our resources to look into it myself."

Artemis frowned at him. "I suppose the reason you want to help is because you think that'll indebt me to you and the FBI."

He shook his head. He was frowning now. "Look, I'd be lying if I said I don't have my own interests in mind. But, on the other hand..." He hesitated and for a moment looked as if he was going to stop talking. But then, in a quieter voice, his eyes distant, he murmured, "you remind me of someone..."

She frowned. His tone had gone strangely deadpan. His expression emotionless.

As he nodded and glanced off past her, it almost felt as if he forgot she was standing there. Forester didn't usually have much emotion to communicate. But she was stunned to hear the faintest tremor to his voice. Something else she had noticed about sociopaths when reading online. Most of them couldn't make normal emotional connections. But sometimes, sociopaths could choose one or two core people that they eventually grew very close to. They wouldn't form attachments with almost anyone else. But when they did form the rarest of attachments, to someone critical in their lives, usually over the course of years, they would treat them like royalty. She couldn't quite imagine what it would be to live a life without emotion. Without affection. But there, in that brief glimpse, it almost felt like Forester's voice quavered with something bordering grief.

She stared at him, feeling a jolt of pity.

He cleared his throat and shook his head. "Doesn't matter. I don't mean to make you uncomfortable," he added quickly. He gave a quick grin. "My mother used to have panic attacks, you know."

Artemis nodded. "You said it before."

He scratched at his messy hair, but began to turn. "Think about it. If you decide to work long term, Grant would probably do you a solid on this one." He shrugged as he left and waved a hand over his shoulder. "It's at least worth considering."

And then he stomped away, down the hall, disappearing along another bend.

She frowned after him shaking her head. A very strange man. She wasn't sure it was safe to consider making a man like that a colleague.

Then again, dealing with her father, her sister, or with her home-town wouldn't be safe.

And now she had a more proximate reason to get into the FBI's good graces. Cynthia had lost her grandson. And there was something Artemis could do about it. Was this the push she needed? The straw that broke the camel's back?

It wasn't like she was signing her life away. She could help out on a couple of cases now and then. She found it invigorating. It helped her keep her mind agile. And most importantly, it would give her access to case files on Helen's disappearance and her father's record.

Information she had been avoiding. Running from. The only things she really knew about the case from fifteen years ago were because of online articles she read.

That could change. Forester's motives were suspect.

But, she decided, choices like that could wait until morning.

7

Matthieu shifted nervously in his new car. The fresh scent of the vehicle wafted on the air but competed with another, stronger scent of aftershave. Matthieu winced, rolling down the window and giving a quick surreptitious sniff at his shirt.

Too much. The scent was too strong.

Panicked, he tried to run through his options. This was only going to be their third date... and everyone knew what that meant.

He rolled down the second window, trying to create a cross-breeze and air his car out. Matthieu sat in an isolated, private portion of the Martan Arboretum, beneath an old tree that towered into the air.

Matthieu adjusted the small box of chocolates balanced on the dashboard. Lucy loved chocolates. But at the store, he'd forgotten if she liked milk or dark. Or maybe she preferred one of those toffee crunch things. In a panic, he had bought all three.

And now, he shifted restlessly, swallowing uncomfortably at the thought.

He could still detect the odor of aftershave.

A small stream trickled by in front of him, between the trees.

The arboretum, this early in the morning, was usually quiet. The first glimmers of sunlight crested across the horizon. His aunt worked for the arboretum and so had given him special access a few minutes before the park was supposed to open.

Now, as he watched a dragonfly buzz over the stream, he heard the sound of a snapping branch.

He looked up, excited.

He tried to smooth his hair, brushing it quickly out of his eyes.

He really liked Lucy. The fact that she had agreed to meet him here, even for their third date, told him that she also wanted some privacy.

He smiled at the thought. He was only one year out of high school, having graduated early. Most of his school career had been a lonely one.

But now, he was finding that quiet, shy and nice were not quite the detriment he'd initially supposed.

He checked in the mirrors, glancing towards the trail.

For a moment, he wondered if he ought to turn the radio on. Would she like music? Maybe not.

He thought better of it, muttering to himself. "Don't be stupid."

He cleared his throat, made a couple of desperate scooping motions with his hand as if to wand the air from the car.

And then, he opened the door, pushing out and stepping onto the leaf strewn ground.

He smiled towards the trail.

A figure stepped off the path, moving behind the tree.

He hesitated, quizzically.

"Lucy?" he said, still smiling. Quickly, he adjusted his expression. He didn't want her to think he was too eager.

He swallowed, quickly rubbing his clammy hands against his thighs. Should he shake her hand? Hug her?

The first two dates they had simply nodded in greeting and smiled.

He was awkward. He knew that. What was the etiquette on the third date?

Were they going to kiss?

Crap. He had forgotten to brush his teeth. Did he have mints?

Why, for God's sake, hadn't he brought mints?

He tried to refocus, swallowing and staring towards the trail. "Lucy?" he said, a bit more hesitantly now.

He took a step towards the large tree. Some of the branches hung low, extending towards him.

He shifted from one foot to the other. And then, his phone buzzed. Frowning, he lifted the device and studied the notification.

"I'm running late."

A message from Lucy.

He stared at his phone. Then looked sharply up again at the tree behind which the stranger had darted.

A cold shiver trembled up his spine.

The arboretum was open to the public. But this early, with the gates only having recently been open to the public, it was rare for people to visit this particular spot on the two-thousand-acre preservation. In fact, he had specifically chosen this location because of how isolated it was.

He heard another snap of a twig. The rustle of leaves. The crunch of footsteps.

He swallowed shakily. "Hello?" he said slowly.

There were some gardeners who worked throughout the arboretum. Usually older men who were retired.

He couldn't say exactly why, but the shiver along his arms and his neck was now spreading to the tips of his fingers. His palms buzzed.

"Hello?" he said, louder, his voice shaking.

And then someone stepped from behind the tree. The figure was wearing a hood, dark clothing.

But he didn't quite have the chance to take in their appearance.

Rather, his attention was fully riveted by the gun clutched in the figure's hand, pointed directly at him.

"Don't move," a voice said, low and husky. "Do exactly what I say."

He swallowed, gaping. He stammered and took a stumbling step back. For a moment, he thought to turn and run, but it was as if his legs were glued to the ground.

He heard a faint zipping sound. A backpack hooked over the other arm, placed on the ground now. The gun still pointed at him. And then, from the backpack, through an unzipped compartment, a long coil of rope emerged, clutched tight in a gloved hand.

8

Artemis cleared her throat, looked Forester dead in the eyes, and said, "I've been thinking about it, and I'd like to take you up on your offer for help."

It was her turn to stand outside his hotel door.

Forester's hair was wet and jutting in every direction. He wore the same T-shirt he had the night before, but parts were damp, sticking to an impressive physique. Forester's muscled form displayed the faintest outline of scars just beneath his shirt. The damp portions of the fabric helped to mold the injured skin.

"So you're taking Grant up on the offer?" Forester said, raising an eyebrow and running a hand through his hair. Flecks of water scattered and flashed across the backdrop of illumination provided by bright beams of sunlight flaring through the open window behind the agent.

Artemis clutched her phone tightly. She had already notified Mrs. Washington of the day's itinerary. Cynthia was still trying to coax her husband from his stupor, but she had managed to provide Artemis with a name.

"Maverick Anthony," Artemis said, simply.

"What?"

"Maverick Anthony," she said, more insistently. "I need you to look up the name for me."

"You're sure that's not just some sports car?"

"That's the name of the teenager that Henry Rodine put in the hospital. Blinded him in one eye."

Forester winced, scratching at his chin. "I'm not sure I'm allowed to use FBI resources if you're not officially consulting. You still haven't answered my question. What do you think about Grant's offer?"

Artemis sighed. "I don't know, Cameron. It's a big commitment."

"It's not like she's asking you to marry her; it's just a couple of months of training. Helping out on a few cases on a consultant basis. It basically puts your name on a list and allows us to give you a call when we need some help."

She sighed and nodded. "I understand. Still, I don't know."

Forester frowned. "Like I said, I'm not sure I can help you." He turned and grabbed a towel draped over a desk chair, running it rough against his head. He dropped it behind the chair and turned away, facing the mirror over his desk and poking at a bruise along his collar bone.

Artemis had grown accustomed to seeing Forester with bruises and scrapes and cuts. She'd learned to stop asking about them.

Now, though, as he probed gingerly at his collar bone, she said, "Just this once. I need to know where I can find this guy. That's it."

"I'll make you a deal." He looked back over at her, frowning. There was no humor in his tone. His eyes narrowed. "You tell me how your dad knew what he did, and I'll tell you who this Maverick guy is."

Artemis winced. "I," she hesitated, swallowed. "I don't know."

"How don't you know?"

"I mean I don't know how he found out that information."

He turned, crossing his arms, his muscles standing out against the thin fabric of his T-shirt. "Is it because he's psychic? He really is, isn't he? You just don't want to admit it."

She sighed, tapping her fingers uncomfortably against her phone. She slipped the device into her pocket, left it there for a few seconds and then, as if it were some sort of security blanket, grabbed it again and pulled it out just to hold it. "No," she said, slowly. "There is no such thing. I would tell you if he was psychic. Forester, my dad is up to something. He's bringing information in from the outside with the help of Joseph Baker. He's been getting postcards."

"Right," said Forester slowly. "The postcards. You haven't found anything else about them, have you?"

She shook her head. "No, I haven't. But I'm still looking. In fact, the people who were helping me with the postcards," she said slowly, feeling a sudden epiphany, "are the ones who lost their grandson. If you help me on this case, they would probably be willing to help us figure out how my father is communicating with the postcards." Then, increasing in volume and speed, she finished with a flourish of, "In fact, maybe one of the cards gives information about you. You might be able to find out exactly how and what he knows."

For her part, she felt her own curiosity piqued. Part of her wanted to ask Forester exactly what her father had been hinting at the last time they'd visited him in prison, but now wasn't the time.

She swallowed slowly, wanting to add more but deciding she had made her case. She didn't know what those postcards held. Didn't know what her father was up to or how he was getting his information.

But she did know that the next lead in the case would be to look at Maverick Anthony.

Forester lowered his arms now, shaking his head. "You drive a hard bargain, Checkers. Fine. I'll look up this guy. If I get shit for it, though, I'm blaming you. I'm telling Grant you lied to me. You promised you were going to join. Train with us. If you don't, she's going to take it personally."

Artemis hesitated. "Deal. You can tell her whatever you want. Just so long as you know the truth."

Forester shrugged once then reached out with both arms and pulled his T-shirt off, revealing a muscled, trim physique.

Artemis blinked in surprise. She turned away sharply, her cheeks reddening. She felt a warm flush and shook her head. "I'll wait for you downstairs."

"Oh, I don't mind. I'm just going to be a second."

But Artemis reached out, grabbed the door handle, and closed it slowly.

Then she turned and hastened away. As she walked in the opposite direction of the hotel room door, she realized this was the second time Forester had stood half naked in front of her in a hotel. Coincidence? Or intentional?

This, she felt, was just another reason to be cautious around Forester.

Her skin buzzed and her fingers drummed against her legs. For some reason, her mind moved to Jamie Kramer. She thought about the message she had sent. She still hadn't responded to the voicemail.

He had sounded so alone. She knew exactly what it was to feel alone.

So, prompted by a jolt of sympathy, she pulled her phone out, scrolled to his number, and hastily texted back. *Everything going all right. In Chicago. I got a job offer in Seattle.* She hesitated here, frowning. And then, quickly, she said, *Think I should take it?*

She stared at the message for a second—what did it matter if Jamie Kramer thought she should take a job based in Seattle. She didn't want to return to Pinelake. Didn't want to return to Seattle.

At least, she'd spent half her life telling herself this.

But more and more was dragging her back to her old stomping grounds.

It was as she hastened down the stairs towards the atrium of the hotel lobby, that she made a quiet vow to herself.

If she was able to solve this case, if she was able to *prove* that Henry really was innocent of everything and had nothing to do with the murder, then she would look into Helen's disappearance. Then she would take the job in Seattle. She would train with the FBI and work as a consultant, while playing chess full time. And she would use every resource she could to find out what had happened seventeen years ago.

If there was hope for Henry, then there was hope for Helen.

She nodded to herself, determinedly, taking the stairs two at a time, her hand extended, grazing along the smooth lacquer of the railing.

This was the prompting she needed. She would leave it up to fate.

If she solved the case, she was going back to Seattle. She was going to find her sister. And she was going to figure out what her father was up to and stop him.

But if she couldn't solve the case, then it would be evidence that it was best to let sleeping dogs lie.

And with this determination, Artemis picked up her pace, moving towards the counter at the base of the stairs to wait for Forester to join her and look up the information she needed about the man Henry Rodine had put in the hospital.

9

Artemis looked up from a row of postcards in the hotel gift shop, glancing as Agent Forester approached her with long strides. He shot a quick look at the postcards then frowned at her. "I looked up Mr. Anthony."

Artemis lowered a laminated card into a white wired slot. She turned, frowning. "Why do you look worried?"

"You can't go and speak with him."

"Umm, why not?"

Forester shook his head. "Trust me. It's not a good idea."

Artemis placed a hand on her hip, her elbow cocked. "Why not?" she said, more insistently.

Forester was wearing his suit again. This time, he hadn't even bothered with the buttons. At least his shoes now matched.

The tall agent said, "Maverick Anthony is the son of Carter Anthony." Artemis stared blankly as Forester continued. "Carter Anthony is a longtime guest of Naperville's maximum-security."

Artemis hesitated. "What's your point?"

Forester said, "Maverick currently lives with his uncles. Three of them. His oldest uncle, his father's brother, is named Knuckles."

"Really?"

"Really. Knuckles Anthony has been arrested for murder on two separate occasions but released when witnesses key to the case vanished."

Artemis crossed her arms now, feeling the soft fabric of her sweater. She preferred wearing long sleeves, but because the sweater had been purchased in the hotel gift shop, it was a couple sizes too large.

"So you're saying Henry injured and hospitalized the son of a career criminal whose uncle is a suspected murderer?"

"Not just his uncle. All three of his uncles. They live in the same house. A giant mansion near the local arboretum." Forester shook his head. "Like I said, steer clear. I know you're being a good friend, but you should probably leave this one up to the professionals."

Artemis moved away from the rack of postcards, frowning. "The professionals," she said testily, "have closed the case. And they're wrong."

Forester shrugged. "Well, at the very least, you can't go alone."

She watched him closely. "You want to come with?"

He sighed. "What would I tell Grant if her prodigy ended up dead in a ditch?"

Artemis shook her head. "I imagine that would be an uncomfortable conversation."

"I talked to Grant. Desmond is staying in Seattle. She's still waiting on an answer from you about the job offer but asked me to remind you that you only have a couple of days left."

Artemis nodded. "I remember; does she know you're staying?"

Forester shrugged. "No. I told her I was taking the next flight back."

"You know, normally people think twice about lying to their family members."

Forester wrinkled his nose. "It's not like I'm hurting her. I'm here to help. Besides, she was the one who wanted me to babysit her prospective employee." He studied her, hands in his pockets now. "Do you want me to come with or not?"

Artemis felt a flash of gratitude at the offer. It was so hard to read the motives behind Forester's choices. A part of her suspected he wanted what most men did. Another part of her wondered if he had been telling the truth the previous night. She reminded him of someone. Someone that had mattered to him. Another part of her wondered if this was just a long con on behalf of Agent Grant, trying to convince her to join the FBI. As a long-term consultant, she would have increased access to information but also increased responsibilities and time commitments, and a willingness to put herself in harm's way.

She sighed slowly "I'm not going to say no. Thanks."

Forester nodded once, flashing a quick thumbs up with his scarred hand.

He said, "Good. Because I extended my stay for another night. We can take my car, if you want. Just," he said, slowly, "let me do the talking."

She stared at him. "Forester, when you talk, people try to shoot you."

He nodded. "It's part of my charm. At the very least let me do the introductions. Credentials get you through more doors than you think. Besides, a lady like you, with that innocent little face, they'd eat you alive."

He shook his head and began to move away, heading towards the front doors of the hotel, moving quickly.

She shifted uncomfortably at these last words.

The next step made sense. If there was someone motivated to kill Henry and his girlfriend, it could very easily have been the son of a criminal. Especially the son of a violent criminal. If it was true that Henry had hospitalized Maverick, then that could explain the grisly nature of the crime scene.

But also, things were starting to feel more dire.

A house full of known criminals wasn't exactly the same thing as creeping into an abandoned home in the dead of night.

She sighed, glancing at her phone, and quickly texted Mrs. Washington. *"We have a lead. I'll keep you posted."*

She sent the message quickly.

Jamie Kramer still hadn't replied to her previous text. She imagined he was probably busy sending Sophie off to school.

She followed Agent Forester out of the sliding doors.

The one question she didn't quite know how to answer was what if she was right? What if the Anthony family was behind the double murder? How did that tie them to the other case Forester had found? Some sort of organized crime thing? An attempt to disguise the real reason behind a murder?

It wasn't like people took murder accusations very lightly. Especially not known criminals who were likely to be heavily armed.

She swallowed, feeling exposed all of a sudden, and picked up her pace to catch up with Forester where he was unlocking his rented vehicle.

***

Artemis stared up at the enormous mansion, her jaw unhinged. She had never seen a house so large. It spread in every direction, as if it were some living thing, like ivy or moss sending roots and shoots out to conquer more space. The garage alone with four red-painted aluminum doors was larger than most houses.

There was a tall metal fence circling the house.

In fact, as she stared at the enormous stone structure with a wooden deck circling the side of the house and overlooking a large pool, she felt as if the two-story home might even have been larger than the hotel she'd stayed at the previous night.

"Now that's a certain type of money," Forester murmured beneath his breath.

She just nodded.

"Remember, let me do the talking."

Artemis frowned, shooting a look at Forester. He had parked on a smooth, black, asphalt driveway. They faced large, golden letters on the gate, which in cursive displayed the initials CA.

Multiple stone columns held up a terrace the size of most court-yards.

A couple of vehicles with bright red paint resembled spaceships more than automobiles. These were parked under a shade screen extending from the fourth door of the garage.

There weren't very *many* trees inside the gate. Almost no flowers. And the grass was mostly brown. But still, the impressive spectacle couldn't help but draw the eye.

Artemis tilted her head, listening, and frowned in the direction of the garage.

"Hear that?" she said slowly.

Forester followed her gaze, frowning and adjusting his suit. He had managed to button it correctly this time. A rarity. Mostly, as she had watched him fumble with the buttons while driving towards their destination, it had seemed as if he hadn't cared.

Often, when spending time with Forester, she felt as if he were something of a free spirit crammed into a suit against his will.

Now, though, as they sat in their vehicle, facing the large gates outside the mansion, he perked up with interest.

He hesitated for a second, glanced at the keys in the ignition, then glanced up again.

Artemis went still. "Hang on," she said quickly. "Wait, let's not—"

But Forester pushed out of the vehicle.

He hesitated, frowned, and reached back inside the car, twisting the keys and removing them.

He jangled the keys in her direction with a knowing look, and then turned back to face the garage, peering between the metal bars.

Artemis sighed. The last time she had been left alone in a running car, a known murderer had hijacked it and taken her with it. Only after some quick thinking had she managed to get the convict to drive the vehicle right back to where they'd started.

Now, she huffed in frustration. Forester was walking towards the fence.

She stepped out of the car as well. Not because she particularly wanted to, but because this had been her idea.

Mrs. Washington had texted back earlier.

Every now and then, Artemis' phone would buzz with a new question about how she was doing. If she was safe. And if there was anything Cynthia could do.

But right now, the only thing Artemis could think was for Mrs. Washington to stop with the texting. But she didn't want to offend the woman, so instead, Artemis had put her phone on silent.

Now, standing outside the vehicle, feeling the sunlight against her skin, she could hear a distinct sound coming from the garage.

Music.

Heavy, pounding, clashing music.

"Forester," she whispered. "There's a camera."

Agent Forester glanced towards the camera over the gate. He wrinkled his nose and shook his head. "No wires," he said.

She frowned. "I'm pretty sure it's possible to have a battery-operated camera," she said firmly.

He shook his head. "Nah, it's probably a dud. I'm going to check out the sound."

Artemis hesitated. She glanced curiously at the security camera, back at Forester, then up again. "Forester, I'm nearly certain that you can have a battery—"

But he wasn't listening. She realized, a second later, he was probably just answering her questions in order to get her to stop talking.

Now, he was climbing up the fence.

She felt a jolt of envy, remembering her own escapade the night before. Forester took far less hip shimmying and wiggling. He managed to reach the top, slipped over, and dropped down the other side with a couple of quick, athletic motions.

Artemis frowned at him, glanced at the gate, then back at the long driveway.

She hesitated for a second then approached the gate.

Forester watched her curiously through the bars.

She pressed a number on the keypad.

There was a buzz, and a red light flickered.

She frowned and tried another number. This time another buzz. Another red light flickered.

She tried a third combination. A green light. A *click*. The two gates began to slowly open.

Artemis dusted her hands off, and, nonchalantly as possible, still feeling a faint shiver down her spine, she moved through the gates.

Forester stared right at her. "What did you do?"

She replied, "I used the gate code."

Forester glanced at the fence he climbed, then the open gate, then Artemis. "I don't care what you say, I know you're psychic."

She sighed. "I tried the house address. I tried Mr. Anthony's birth year. And then I tried the date when his brother is supposed to get out of prison from the file on your phone."

"The oh... That's what you were looking at, I thought you were programming the GPS. Shit, Checkers, I'm pretty sure that's a breach of national security or something for you to go through an agent's phone." He said this as if he couldn't care in the least.

She shrugged.

But he had turned again and was now moving slowly, cautiously, across an asphalt driveway, beneath a basketball hoop.

A deflated, weathered ball rested in the prickling, brown grass at the edge of the square of tarmac.

Forester stepped over the ball and approached the garage where the loud sounds were coming from.

Artemis followed slowly.

She shot another look towards the giant mansion. If it came to it, she wondered how long it might take to find someone hiding in a place like that.

Forester reached towards his hip, unbuttoning his holster.

Artemis stared, swallowing a lump in her throat. The grass almost felt crunchy underfoot. Whoever the gardener was, they had clearly neglected their job.

She moved up the driveway, towards the fourth door of the garage. The sounds were coming loudest from here. There was a single window set above the garage door.

Forester hesitated, frowning at the window. He looked around for a moment, clearly searching for something to stand on.

But then, instead, Forester took a note out of Artemis' book. He reached down, grabbed the edge of the metal, aluminum sliding door, and lifted sharply with a grunt.

His arms strained as he pulled the door up.

Artemis went still, staring past the agent into the garage.

The music blared now, no longer muffled by the closed door.

She stared into the garage, eyes landing on a row of mirrors, reflecting over racks of weights and dumbbells. A few exercise machines lined the left side of the space. On the right side, there was a rowing machine and a barbell rack.

And there, resting on the barbell bench, was a young man who looked like a bodybuilder.

He wasn't very large, more compact. But his muscles were pronounced, veins bulging, arms rippling as he pumped iron. Up, down, Artemis watched, mesmerized as the weights lifted and lowered.

The man was wearing a sleeveless T-shirt. He had on sweatpants and sneakers. As he pumped the weights, he was moving in rhythm to the loud music blaring through the garage. Sweat slicked his arms and his forehead. Some of the sweat covered the ground, staining the black rubber matting.

He was breathing heavily, huffing as he lifted the bar and lowered it.

"Mr. Anthony?" Forester called.

The young man didn't seem to hear. He continued working out.

Artemis watched as he reached the pinnacle of the final press, his arms straining.

"Mr. Anthony?" Forester said, louder.

The song was beginning to fade. By the looks of things, the young man had timed his workout to the music. When the music died, his exercise stopped.

Now, though, as he was straining to finish his final set, lifting the barbell high, the weights straining above him, he tensed and looked sharply up.

He yelped, and the heavy workout equipment slipped.

Forester cursed, sprinting forward as the barbell shifted sideways and toppled.

One side of the heavy plates hit the ground, scoring a mark into the rubber. The other side, though, swung down, and the man working out managed to catch it with his fingers.

The heavy weights tilted towards his neck, and he strained, groaning, trying to prevent it from falling on his chest or throat.

Forester reached the barbell a second later, grabbed it, and ripped it off.

"Sorry, man," Forester said quickly. "Didn't mean to spook you."

The young man was gasping, sitting up now and trying to recover. Sweat poured down his face. He shot wide-eyed looks of panic at Artemis and Forester. He swallowed a few times as he stared at the agent. He looked younger even than when she had first spotted him. His hair was brushed back, held by a headband. His forehead was pockmarked from acne scars.

Also, as his eyes darted back and forth between them, Artemis realized the left eye was stationary.

She stared, and the thing stared back. Without moving, it reflected the light from the bulbs in the ceiling in a strange, glinting way.

There was a scar along the underside of his eye, stretching down his cheek.

The young man cursed, rising off the bench and stumbling back, away from them.

"Hang on," Forester said quickly. "Don't panic. FBI!" He raised his badge in a self-assured sort of way.

The young man stared and then began to shout. "Cops! Cops in the garage!"

He darted forward and reached for the dumbbell rack.

It took Artemis a second, though, to realize he was trying to grab something wedged between two of the heavier metal weights.

A gun.

"Forester!" she shouted.

The agent cursed, darting forward. He shoved the man away from the gun. Now, Artemis felt fairly certain, given the eye injury, that this was Maverick Anthony.

He yelled as he stumbled to the ground.

He tried to rise, but Forester pushed him with his foot, sending him sprawling. At the same time, Forester grabbed the gun from where it was wedged between the dumbbells and slipped it into his waistband in one smooth motion.

"Stay on the ground!" Forester snapped.

It was like watching someone take off a mask. One moment, Forester had been curious, jovial even. But now, the second the man had reached for the gun, Forester had turned brittle. His eyes narrowed, and his jaw clenched. Forester's hands had formed fists, and one of his hands lingered near his own holster.

Artemis glimpsed his reflection in the large mirrors.

Forester inhaled slowly, exhaled.

For a moment, his eyes didn't blink as he stared at the man on the ground.

Artemis was trying to read his body language. Trying to keep track of everything, as a sort of coping mechanism of her own. Otherwise, the panic would have simply inoculated her from use.

But now, as her eyes darted around, she couldn't make out much of Forester's emotions.

He didn't seem angry. Didn't seem scared. If anything, he seemed deadpan. Indifferent. But cold.

That was the best word for it. Very, very cold.

She remembered that same expression from back when her father had been interrogated. When her father had taunted Forester about whatever had transpired all those years ago. Now, as Forester stared at Maverick, it was as if he was seeing someone else.

"Stay down," Forester said, his tone as chill as ice.

10

The young man tried to protest, still gasping, his sweat slicked body leaving marks against the black, rubber padding on the floor.

"We just wanted to chat," Forester said, growling. "No need to reach for a piece. Are you Maverick?"

The young man nodded quickly. His one working eye still darting around.

And then, Artemis heard shouting. Footsteps.

She turned, looking sharply over her shoulder and going suddenly still.

Three more men were charging down from the house, weapons in their hands, pointing at the garage and shouting.

Two of the men were wearing sleeveless shirts, just like Maverick. They didn't look much older. One of the men, though, was in a strange outfit.

He wore no shirt. His hands were jammed into two gloves, red, thick. He had bright, shining shorts. Tattoos carved his chest, his arms, branding every available inch of his skin.

Artemis stared, mouth agape.

The one with the boxing gloves was shouting, "Get away from him. Get away!" There was fear in his voice.

The other two had firearms raised, pointing towards the garage.

"Forester!" Artemis said, loud. She was beginning to regret allowing him to come along.

"Hang on," Forester snapped. He took three quick steps to the side, his hand lashing out, and hitting a switch on the wall. The aluminum door began to slowly creek and rattle. It rolled along the track and then began to lower, slowly.

Artemis winced as Forester yelled, "Get away from the door!"

There were no gunshots, yet. Artemis hoped this was because they were worried about hitting their kin.

She hadn't seen the pictures of the men who lived in the mansion, but she remembered what Forester had said. Uncles. All of them related to Maverick. The oldest of the brothers, Maverick's father, was still in prison.

Artemis took a few shuffling steps to the side, out of line of sight from the lowering door.

The last glimpse she had of the three sprinting men was the wide, whites of their eyes as they stared towards where Maverick was prone on the ground.

As the door rattled shut, Artemis found a hand tugging insistently at her. "Here, hold this. Point that way. Pull the trigger if they start shooting."

Artemis felt a jolt of terror as cold metal was pressed into her hands. She stared down, gaping at the weapon.

"I-I," she stammered. "I don't know how..."

Forester gave her a hard pat on her shoulder. "Learn on the fly, Checkers. You—yeah, you, buddy with the glass eye, get up!"

Forester was now gesturing urgently towards the sweaty man on the ground.

Maverick couldn't have been much older than twenty. He was glaring belligerently where Forester postured over his prone form.

"You're gonna get got," Maverick said, eyes narrowed. He jutted a Flintstone chin towards the agent. "Think you're smart? You got a smart mouth."

Forester nodded along with the comments as if interested. Then, when Maverick took a moment to draw breath, Forester said, "You done?"

"You stupid, piece of—"

Forester yanked him to his feet, holding him by the collar of his sleeveless shirt and directing him towards the door.

He gestured quickly with his own gun. "Artemis, behind me please."

Artemis' hands were shaking so badly she nearly dropped the weapon. Loud voices yelled on the other side of the corrugated, metal door. She heard pounding of fists. And then, a sliver of light beneath the door, accompanied by prying fingers trying to yank the door up.

"Artemis, behind me," Forester said, a bit more urgently. His eyes were narrowed again. The same coldness lingering. He didn't sound scared, didn't look perturbed. He just stared at the opening door with a quiet air of inevitability. He kept Maverick between them and the door as Artemis scampered back. She tried her best to keep a grip on her weapon.

Safety... Wasn't that what always happened in the movies? Someone left their safety on?

What in the hell was a safety?

She stared at the gun, wincing. Not that it mattered—she wasn't about to shoot anyone.

"M-maybe I should talk," she said, her voice tremoring.

Forester shot a look at her. "You're pale as a sheet, Checkers. Try to stay standing, alright?"

Artemis was breathing heavily now.

Forester shot her a look. His cold expression flickered, if only briefly. "Deep breaths," he murmured. "It's fine. We're fine, alright, calm down?"

"You ain't fine," snapped the young man gripped by Forester. "My uncles are gonna rip you to pieces."

Forester shook Maverick, hard, sending more sweat drops scattering across the floor.

"Dude, you stink," Forester said. "Just shut up, alright?"

But any repartee was lost as the door to the garage was suddenly yanked open.

Sunlight streamed back through, joining the faux illumination provided by the bright bulbs in the ceiling. Six shadows of long legs stretched through the door, cast by the sun, eventually culminating in silhouettes cast towards the three figures in the workout room.

Finally, with a grunt, one of the men in a sleeveless shirt pushed the metal door into the ceiling.

Now, all three of them faced the interior of the garage.

The man with the boxing gloves was quickly tearing at them with his teeth. With a sound of ripping Velcro, he finally managed to dislodge one, tossing it to the ground. He made quicker work of the second one, now with the use of his fingers.

The man jabbed a finger straight at Forester. The finger glinted nearly the same way Maverick's eye did, but this was due to the pearlescent rings looping along three of his fingers in a strange display of odd ornamentation.

Artemis didn't like the feeling of hiding behind Forester, but she also didn't like the feeling of holding the gun. She was pointing it off towards the mirror in order to avoid the risk of accidentally hurting anyone.

The two men in the door didn't have any such aversions. They pointed their firearms directly at Forester and Artemis, scowling deeply, each of them uglier than the other.

The man who'd discarded the gloves was now pulling a switchblade from his pocket, flashing it towards them and twisting a lip into a snarl.

He had a youthful face, but crow's feet in the corners of his eyes. One of his tattoos stretched up under his chin, over his eyebrow and ended in a pitchfork like a devil's trident.

The man with the pitchfork tattoo had a thick beard that hid most of his pronounced jaw, and both of his ears were lumpy like Forester's.

Artemis noted a pair of swinging silver boxing gloves on a chain around his throat, bouncing off his chest.

The man pointed his switchblade at Forester as he took a few steps into the garage, still scowling.

"Uh-uh," Forester cautioned, shaking his gun side to side. "I like my personal space, boys, let's just chat, can we? I'm a fed."

"Don't give a shit if you're the president," snapped the man with the face tattoo. "You're trespassing, and you've got a gun to my nephew's skull. Drop your piece, or I'll drop you, Stretch."

Forester hesitated, then, his tone still cold, he said, "Technically, the gun is *next* to your nephew's head. But it's pointed at *you*. So why don't we all calm down a bit and share our feelings before anyone gets ventilated."

Three sets of angry eyes had now moved from Artemis and fixated on Forester, who was currently serving as a bit of lightning rod.

Artemis shifted uncomfortably, swallowing as she watched the men glance at each other, scowling.

"We—we just wanted to ask some questions!" Artemis piped up, summoning what nerve she had. Nearly instantly, she wished she'd kept her cool. She winced uncomfortably as everyone now glanced in her direction. Even Maverick shot a look into the tall mirror to study her out of the corner of his eye.

Artemis shifted uncomfortably. "Umm... Just... we... wanted to ask you about..." She wasn't sure what protocol was in these scenarios. Her mind was flaring with panic. Her stomach tightening. Normally, she would ask questions to people who weren't inches away from filling her with lead. Now, she felt a slow prickle of fear along her back.

She tried her best not to hyperventilate, her breath coming in quick puffs as she attempted to settle her nerves. She tried to focus, to zero in on the figures in the garage doorway. Now, as she studied them, she winced. Her mind darted to the thin dusting of powder along the hem of the boxer's trousers. Suggesting he had wiped his fingers off earlier, but a faint residue of white dust lingered.

The two other men had red-ringed eyes, both looking panicked. Their nostrils flared as they breathed, and their motions were twitchy, fidgety. Every few moments, they shot quick glances towards the man with the knife standing above the discarded, red boxing gloves as if searching for some type of cue.

A few things were obvious. Two of them were high. The third one, with the boxing shorts, wasn't sweating, which meant he'd only *just* been gearing up for sparring practice or a workout—whatever he'd intended. Now, the man standing by the gloves also boasted a metal chain around his neck. Artemis had heard of *golden* gloves before, but she'd never seen the silver type.

However, she did spot a tattoo that stood out to her. It simply read *Knuckles "The Brick" Anthony.*

She stared at the tattoo, and then her eyes darted up to the man in charge. He was the linchpin, the other two would do exactly what he said. And now, as guns flashed, eyes glared and postures tensed, she took a shot of her own.

Instead of relying on bullets, though, she used information...

...and body language.

She instantly lowered her gun, her eyes widening. She stared directly at the face of the boxer, careful not to even glance towards the tattoo lest she give away the source of her information.

The key with any sort of mental trick was to keep multiple possible outcomes held loosely. The best tricks were *not* ones where the result was predetermined. But, rather, ones where the result was *faked* to be predetermined.

It had the exact same sense of awe in an audience, but didn't cost nearly as much preparation.

Her father's bread and butter had been switching tricks halfway through.

"Oh my!" she exclaimed. "I *knew* it was you. You're the Brick, aren't you?" She widened her eyes in surprise. "Mind if I get a picture?"

The two men with red-ringed eyes blinked in confusion. But the one with the boxing gloves glared at her. "What the hell are you talking about?"

She kept her wide-eyed look fixed in place, refusing to let it slip. Even a crack in the facade would be like a whimper of fear in the face of a grizzly attack. But not all posturing was threatening.

A man like this, a man who commanded the respect of his brothers, who lived in a *giant* home like this, who wore his accolades around his neck in the form of boxing gloves, was someone who *craved* attention and approval.

People like this were easy enough to spot. If even for a second they thought you were manipulating them, though, things could get downright dangerous.

But up *until* that point?

Other levers could be pulled.

Artemis was tapping Forester on the shoulder now. "Oh, come on. Don't be silly—this is *him!* The guy I was telling you about."

Forester hesitated, glancing at her, then back at the men with the guns. He shifted uncomfortably, frowning.

She leaned in, murmuring beneath her breath. "They're high, he's confused. Just do what I say."

Maverick hesitated, scowling into the mirror. He opened his mouth to speak, but Artemis stepped forward, *accidentally* stomping on his foot and speaking over him. Of course, this ruse wasn't exactly banking on out-clevering anyone. But rather, an attempt to defuse tension with confusion.

There was no way that Knuckles Anthony would think she was just some fan who'd accidentally wandered onto his property, with an FBI agent who was now manhandling his nephew.

The focus, the point, was to direct his attention *away* from the obvious conclusions.

It was the same thing with a mugger.

Oftentimes, the best way to distract someone intent on deadly harm was to ask them a *routine* question that required a conditioned and immediate response.

People were trained to instantly respond to certain verbal cues. Everyone was, whether knowingly or not.

And so, as she stepped forward, trying to keep her voice steady and hiding her hands at her sides so they wouldn't see just how pale and shaky they were, she said, "Oh—what time is it?"

She said it firmly, a demand.

The men hesitated, briefly, shifting. The one with the knife blinked, his eyes half darting to a clock on the wall.

All of it was simply to de-escalate. Her father had called it *soothing confusion*.

Another little mentalism trick, forcing a mark's mind into multiple possible trains of thought in order to distract them from a primary emotion. Namely anger, or lust, or greed.

And now, as she stepped forward again, still beaming brightly and smiling, though Forester tried to intercept, the three men with the guns were no longer scowling so much. They looked confused more than anything.

"I saw your last match," Artemis pressed, nodding happily. "You really know how to take a punch."

This was what her father might have called the *lightest lead*. The smallest, nearly useless piece of information. He knew how to take a punch. Judging by the state of his ears, he clearly did. But the claim, the information, was far less useless when hidden towards the end of a play, especially if a mark was confused.

Now, the weapon in her hand had been dropped to the ground.

"This is all just one big misunderstanding," she said cheerfully, though, all she felt was fear. "Why don't we all put our weapons down and talk for a second, hmm? Did you ever box him, Forester? I know you used to be a professional fighter, right?"

This time, the attempt failed. It had been a sloppy try. Establishing a connection. The men were frowning again, their weapons still gripped. But for the moment, Artemis stood somewhat exposed, and they weren't peppering her with bullets.

Baby steps.

The confusion had helped deflate some of the anger. Her cheerful prattle, odd questions, and the sudden knowledge of Knuckles's fighting name had further confused him. The one thing no one wanted to do was to shoot someone they knew but couldn't remember.

She said, "Oh—you don't remember me? We met at that party last week... or was it more than a week ago? Hmm... I think Denise introdu—no, no, it was J... J... what was her name again?"

"Jenine," Knuckles said slowly, still frowning.

"That's right! You gave me the code for your gate," Artemis said. "Told me to stop by... I mean... I guess you might have been wasted at the time."

He frowned at her. "I've been sober three months."

"Oh—you're right. It *was* three months ago. I think one of those nights when you were *really* blacked out." She gave an airy, little laugh, still forcing a calm expression.

Now he looked both confused and curious.

"Oh... Ummm..." He shook his head. "Wait... you're FBI?" he said, scowling at Forester.

Artemis said. "He's a friend of mine. We really were here just to speak with Maverick, actually." It was a difficult thing to try and interrogate someone who was flanked by gun-toting brothers, but she said, anyway, "We wanted to know about Henry Rodine."

The instant she said the name, she watched them all closely, using the mirrors, having gone still and emerged from behind Forester so nothing blocked her line of sight. Most of her attention was fixed on both Knuckles and Maverick. But the other two, who were still gripping their weapons, also warranted a quick glance.

As she scanned the crowd, Artemis' phone suddenly began to vibrate.

The men stared at her. She swallowed, wincing, holding up a finger. The quiet buzzing sound went quiet after a few rings.

Artemis inhaled shakily, refocusing and—

Her phone began to vibrate again.

"Maybe you should take that," Forester muttered in her ear.

Knuckles and his brothers were glaring, seemingly on the verge of action.

Artemis pulled her phone from her pocket and glanced at the name. Cynthia was calling. Artemis winced. It had been a while since she'd updated the woman who'd hired her. But now, Artemis killed the call and pocketed it again.

The men with the guns were still caught between confusion and a desire for sudden action.

But in the mirror, she spotted Maverick flinch at the name. His eyes, including the fake one, narrowing. Knuckles snorted, his chest rising and falling, lifting the silver gloves in one huff of air.

"You're shitting me," he said. "Henry Rodine? You're here about that asshole? What's he done now?"

Forester's weapon was slowly lowering now too. The two men, taking their cue from the tone of their leader were aiming at the floor.

Artemis let out a shaking little breath, making sure her phone was securely back in her pocket. She said, "We'd like to know where you all were two nights ago." She shifted, glancing at the men.

They frowned at her once more. The tension felt thick.

The man with the silver necklace was scowling at Forester now, seemingly deciding that Artemis didn't pose a physical threat. "Hey—let my nephew go, Stretch. I'm not playing."

Forester nodded towards the guns. "How about they drop their clips, and I drop my gun."

Knuckles snorted. He shook his head, suddenly flashing a big, fake grin, displaying silver teeth. "Ah, come on, fed. We were just joking. These are toys anyway."

The weapons certainly looked real enough to Artemis, but she didn't object. Sometimes, a prideful man just needed an exit door. The two men hesitantly lowered their weapons, shoving them into the back of their pants.

Artemis glanced to Forester, expecting him to follow.

Instead, though, the agent pushed Maverick forward, *hard*, sending him stumbling towards his uncle, and then Forester snatched Artemis' weapon from where she'd dropped it. In a swift motion he raised both guns, pointing them at the two men who'd shoved their firearms into their waistbands.

"Twitch, and I drop you," he said simply, unblinking.

Artemis winced. It was a strange thing to see a couple of criminals honor an agreement to lower weapons while the FBI agent didn't. Now, though, the men with the red-ringed eyes were frowning. "Not fair," one of them muttered. "You drop yours, big fellow!"

But Forester made a tutting sound. "Nope, don't do it, bud. I see your hand. Up, up." He waved the weapons.

Artemis took a slow step back, feeling the tension return.

The bare-chested boxer was scowling again. "Below the belt there, Stretch. Think you wanna keep those pointed at my brothers?"

Forester gave a quick nod and a wink. "They're just toy guns, right? Might as well put 'em on the ground, then we can talk all civilized. So go on." He waved both his weapons. "I've shot men for less than aiming a gun at me before. So come on," he said, more insistently, his tone hard. "Weapons on the ground and kick them over."

It took a few motions and more than one muttered expletive as the men complied with the directive. But then, with dark muttering, their weapons finally *clicked* against the hard rubber flooring. Then, one of them kicked his weapon *hard,* and sent it ricocheting off the weight bench. The other one nudged it with his foot, sending it rolling a few times before it landed halfway between them and Forester.

Now Cameron nodded.

"Good job, Artemis," he said cautiously, his eyes still on the men in the garage door.

She wasn't sure how much credit she wanted to take for that. All she wanted was to ask some questions. She wasn't trying to start a shootout.

Then again, she trusted Forester's experience in situations like this.

Forester, though, said slowly, "Don't mean to bend the rules there, boys, but I couldn't help but remember what I saw in your file, Knuckles. Rumor has it those two bodies you bagged happened *after* they turned their backs. Bullets in the spine according to the coroner's report."

Artemis felt a slow chill at these words. She glanced towards Knuckles Anthony who was smirking now. He winked. "Don't know what you're talking about, fed. Think I should have my lawyer present if you're just gonna sling some wild accusations, though."

Forester shook his head, taking a step forward and scooping one of the weapons back, kicking it behind himself. Only then, after a few glances in the mirror, checking to make sure none of the men had anything concealed behind their backs, did he lower his own guns. He holstered his weapon, slowly.

"So," Forester said, "Why don't you answer the nice lady's questions? She's been looking forward to a chat."

Artemis shifted again. "Umm... Yeah... Just—where were you guys? Umm, two nights ago." She swallowed, feeling flustered once more as the attention in the room once again leveled on her.

Everyone shifted a bit, frowning at her.

Knuckles, though, snorted. "I ain't gotta tell you shit, lady."

"He does," Forester said, pointing towards where Maverick was rubbing at his neck, where his shirt collar had been taut. An angry red mark circled his throat. "It's true Henry Rodine did that to your eye?"

Maverick spat off to the side. "Henry got lucky."

"Yeah? How about two nights ago—was he unlucky?" Forester frowned at them.

Maverick paused now, shooting a quick look at his uncle. Knuckles, though, was watching them with a shrewd look in his mean eyes. Then, slowly, he grinned. "Oh, for *real*? Someone capped Henry? Ha! Good riddance. Did it hurt? Tell me the little twerp got bled!"

Maverick looked stunned, staring at his uncle. The two other men didn't look surprised *or* confused. But Artemis wasn't sure if this was because they'd already *known* about the murder, or because they were too high to even track the flow of conversation.

Forester took a step forward now, one gun holstered, the other tucked into his belt. "Why don't you just answer the question," he said. "Where were you all?"

"Couple nights ago?" Knuckles snorted. He gave Forester a once over and then tapped a finger against his chest. "You really a pro?"

"What?"

"A pro—the little lady said you're some type of pro. You know, I coulda gone pro." Knuckles preened now, wiggling his eyebrows and standing tall. He was still a good five inches shorter than Forester, but that didn't seem to matter as he jammed his bearded chin in Cameron's direction.

Forester frowned. "Yeah. I spent some time in the cage. You saying you were at a fight?"

The man shook his head, though. "Nah. I'm not saying that. I'm saying professional fighters ain't got it. You know what I mean? Ain't really scrap. Just overpaid actors is all." He shrugged now, nonchalantly swiping at his nose with the back of his thumb and sniffing. His switchblade had disappeared back into his pocket.

Forester sighed. "You're probably right. You coulda gone pro. The rest of us are scuz. So what do you know about Henry Rodine?"

Maverick, though, was glancing at his uncle, as if trying to read the man's expression. Knuckles reached out, wrapping a hand around the back of his nephew's neck and giving a quick squeeze, equal part affectionate and cautioning. He gave a rough, little push, sending Maverick stumbling away.

Then, the man gave a wave towards the gloves on the ground. "You want answers? How 'bout you earn them? Huh? Big old professional like you."

Forester frowned. "I already said, you'd probably kick my ass. Now why don't you give me *something,* or we might have to have this chat in a colder room with big ol' mirrors."

Knuckles was smirking now, though, nodding as if he'd just discovered the lightbulb. "Yeah... yeah, I like that. Why don't you step up, big guy? Huh? You scared?"

Forester leaned back, exhaling at the ceiling as if exhausted. Quietly, he said, "Let's not, right?"

Knuckles snorted. "You want me to answer *anything,* boss? I'll answer your questions in exchange. You and me. One round. No time. See who's the real fighter." He followed this comment up with a series of quick blows and shots, fist flying, elbow snapping.

Artemis nearly missed it. He moved so fast. She winced, glancing at Forester.

The tall agent sighed. "We're not doing that. You're coming with us. We can do it nice or do it hard."

Knuckles winked. "I like it hard. How 'bout you, hon?" he said, leering at Artemis. "I bet you like it hard too"

"Fine!" Forester snapped. "You want to fight? Let's fight. You lace up first."

Artemis tried to protest, but Knuckles was too busy bending over, chuckling and flexing. "Man, you're in for *a world* of hurt. I'mma red your lips and make you—"

It was as he bent over, chuckling to himself and reaching for a glove, that Forester moved forward.

It wasn't exactly a very *noble* thing. But Artemis was beginning to understand Forester didn't care one *lick* about what others thought. He just tried to get the job done, no matter the cost.

And so, as Knuckles bent over, Forester lunged in *fast*. His foot lashed out, catching their suspect's uncle on the chin. The man's head snapped back, and he didn't even have time to make a sound as he was sent to the ground in a sudden *thump*, like a marionette with severed strings.

It happened so fast—even faster than the mini bout of shadow boxing—so fast that the response from the other men was delayed.

The two uncles yelled suddenly, darting forward, fists raised.

Forester, though, didn't seem to be in the punching mood. Instead, he used the flat of his hand and thumb, jamming it into the throat of the first attacker. There was a sudden sound like a deflating balloon, and the man doubled over, gagging, clutching his throat and gasping at the ground in pain.

The second aggressor tried to swing, but Forester kicked him between the legs *hard*. The man made a sickly sound, his face turning suddenly pale as he toppled over, hands clutching at his groin.

Maverick yelped as Forester pointed at him. "You wanna box too?" Forester said. "I don't think I really know the rules..." He glanced at the three men. Knuckles was completely unconscious.

The two other men were either gasping or groaning on the ground.

Maverick had gone as pale as a sheet and was hastily shaking his head, muttering quick apologies and wincing as he stared at his three uncles.

Forester winced, massaging at his hand quickly, but he hid the expression of discomfort rapidly enough and then gestured at Artemis. "Mind grabbing a couple of my spare cuffs from the car? In the glove compartment. Also, gonna need the radio. Might need a second car to bring these blockheads in."

Artemis just stared for a moment, swallowing slowly and trying to piece together exactly what had happened.

She let out a slow huff of air, staring at where the men writhed or lay strangely still.

Forester had kicked a man in the face while he wasn't watching, had jabbed another man in the throat and then kicked the third in the groin. She wasn't sure what she'd been expecting.

But it certainly wasn't like this in the movies. She shook her head, murmuring softly and shooting a look at the back of Cameron's head. He glanced at her, frowning. "You okay?"

She swallowed, nodding, realizing her hands were trembling again, just as badly as when she'd first seen the gunmen.

But then, at an encouraging but cold-eyed, little nod from the sociopathic law-enforcement officer, Artemis hurried back through the door, careful to sidestep the writhing men and rushing in the direction of the parked vehicle. Only after a few steps did she remember Forester had taken the keys.

She turned quickly, wincing and raising a hand. "Oh—I need—"

But anticipating her request, the keys were already arching mid-air.

She tried to snatch them. But missed, and the keys hit the asphalt.

She sighed, breathing shakily as she grabbed them, picked them up, and hastened towards the parked car.

What had she gotten herself into?

These people... men like this... It was all so uncomfortable. Unusual.

She preferred people who solved their issues with their minds. Not by dropkicking someone's head like a football. She wasn't even sure what to think. How to respond to any of it. She felt another jolt of discomfort as she considered what she'd just witnessed.

The most disturbing part, she felt, was that Forester hadn't seemed to care at all. Even as she'd looked at him, there hadn't been an ounce of distress.

Should there have been? He was just trying to keep her safe, wasn't he?

That was what had triggered his temper. When Knuckles had made the offensive innuendo at her. She swallowed shakily, remembering again what she'd read about sociopaths and their ability to bond with certain people.

You remind me of someone...

She frowned as Forester's words played back through her mind.

Reminded him of *who*?

She shot another look towards the garage where Forester was standing over the fallen men. His sheer force of personality had Maverick rooted to the spot.

Artemis turned away, still shaking, her scalp prickling. This was all too much. Just far too much.

She clicked the locks to the sedan, watching the lights flash through the bars of the gate as she broke into a jog.

11

Artemis felt a bit more comfortable now, standing behind the one-way glass, frowning into the interrogation room. Her skin was still prickling from the altercation back at the Anthony family's mansion. Now, though, she watched as two of the Anthonys settled uncomfortably in the interrogation room, glaring at where Forester sat, across from them.

They were currently an hour from St. Charles, in Rockford. Artemis hadn't been certain, at first, why Forester had insisted on calling for backup and requisitioned aid from a local department so far away.

But over the last hour, she'd gleaned a little.

First, one of Forester's friends was on the force in Rockford. Secondly, the detectives in St. Charles would *not* take kindly to anyone attempting to muscle in on their territory. Artemis had already had an uncomfortable run-in with Detectives Ross and Hardwick. And, she supposed, it made sense not to further irritate them.

For now, at least, the detectives at the St. Charles branch were none the wiser to the altercation.

Forester was his usual, calm self. Again, he had his mischievous, playful tone about him as he spoke with their suspects. Gone was any sign of the cold killer who'd lurked in the garage back outside the mansion. Now that Artemis was safe, that men weren't waving guns, Forester looked downright docile.

Sometimes, his behavior lulled her into a false sense of security. But she had to remember what type of man this really was. She wouldn't make that mistake again.

She stared through the glass now. It had been her idea to put Maverick and his uncle in the same room at the same time.

Forester had agreed, asking her to keep an eye through the one-way window to see if she picked up on anything.

As alarming as the experience back at the mansion garage had been, Artemis had to remember *why* she was here.

Who she was here for?

Mrs. Washington needed answers. Henry's name wasn't cleared yet.

And if ever there was someone who had a grudge and violent capability, it was Maverick's family.

Forester wiggled a small piece of gum towards the two men. "Want one? It's spearmint," he said.

Maverick just stared, his face pale as it had been after watching Forester pummel his uncles. Knuckles, on the other hand, had a giant, foot-sized bruise across his cheek, over his nose and up past an eyebrow. He glared at Forester, sneering. He muttered something beneath his breath that didn't sound very pleasant.

Forester, though, replied with a smile and a nod. "I understand," he said conversationally. "Spearmint isn't my favorite either. Just the only flavor I found in the hotel gift shop." He peeled back the silver wrapper, popped the stick of gum into his mouth, then began chewing.

As he did, he chuckled. "I bet you'd like to know which hotel I'm staying at, huh?"

Knuckles glared.

Forester said, "I didn't *mean* to take it so far, man. I hope you understand. I just get twitchy when people get all rapey. You know?"

Knuckles continued glaring, the effect was somewhat ruined, though, by his black and blue countenance.

Forester leaned back now, shaking his head. "What I can't seem to understand," he said slowly, "is why such a bright, intrepid murderer like yourself has a security camera with *no wires...* crazy right?"

"It's battery powered," Maverick murmured.

Forester wrinkled his nose. "Huh. Well, I owe *someone* an apology." He shook his head. "And so do you, don't you, buddy?" He turned his attention to the younger Anthony now, watching the kid. "Look, little guy, I'm not trying to bust your balls. I'm just trying to figure out what happened to your ol' friend Henry. From what I hear, he's the one who crushed that peeper of yours."

"What?" Maverick said. "You're the one who crushed his—"

"Your eye, Mav," Forester said. "I'm talking about your eye. So what happened? How did Henry bust you up so bad?"

Knuckles snapped. "Lawyer!"

But Maverick was shifting uncomfortably. "It... it wasn't like that," he said. "Henry and I had it out over a girl. I was kicking his ass, too." He shot a quick look at his uncle, nodded as if confirming his own testimony, then continued. "And he was just... you know... an *ass*. He kept coming. And so I tried to give him what was coming and then out of nowhere, man, he just pulls a knife! The little prick was hiding—"

"A little prick? No—no, don't glare. It was funny. That was a joke. If we can't laugh, we can't do anything. Am I right? No? Alright—well, sorry to say, Maverick, I'm not here about what Henry did to you. As you may have heard back there, Henry is dead. And your uncle here doesn't look at *all* broken up about it."

Knuckles shook his head. "He deserved it. Got what was coming. He's just lucky, I didn't find him first."

Forester nodded. "I've been looking at some of that security footage of your little camera by the way. Batteries. I mean, just... wow. How far we've come as a society, am I right? Anyway—looking through some of that stuff, I can't help but notice, Knuckles, you stuck around the old mansion most of the week. What were you hiding from?"

Knuckles shifted uncomfortably. "Nothing," he snapped. "I didn't do anything. If that Rodine kid was wasted, then good riddance. But I didn't do it."

"And what about you, Maverick?" Forester said, glancing at the young man. "What were you up to, two nights ago?"

"I was with Uncle Knuck!" he exclaimed. "I swear! All of my uncles were! It was Uncle Rame's thirty-fifth—"

"Shut up, Mav," his uncle snapped.

Maverick went quiet.

Forester was leaning in now, arms crossed as he stared at the younger man, his gaze fixated on him. "This is some serious stuff, Maverick. If you've got an alibi for the night of the murder, you'd better let me know."

Maverick muttered something but went quiet again after a quick glance at his uncle.

Artemis continued to watch the exchange.

Already, she felt uncertain about how she had acted back at the mansion. She had attempted to confuse and distract the Anthony family, but it had all ended in violence anyway.

Now, as she watched the figures shift uncomfortably on the other side of the glass window, she could feel a slow sense of rising certainty.

They had to separate Maverick's allegiance from his uncle, but she could only think of one way to do that. And it wasn't a very pleasant option.

She wasn't in training. But in a way, it felt like she was undergoing rigorous tutelage. She had been thinking about Forester's violent re-action. At first, it had stunned her. It had bothered her.

Heroes in the movies were not supposed to be underhanded or overly harsh.

But now, faced with the reality of a case, she realized Forester was just doing what he knew.

And in a way, she respected him. Maybe that was her flaw—that she didn't know how to push the envelope. Didn't know how to summon that inner darkness.

Helen had often said everyone had a monster inside. They just had to learn to control it.

When she had found out what her father had done, those words had never been more appropriate.

But now, as she stared through the glass, Artemis could feel some of the mental barriers she had erected slowly dissipate.

She could look at Forester as if he were some sort of bad guy. Or she could join him, knowing that sometimes harsh measures had to be used to yield good results.

She didn't like the choice. Didn't like thinking about people's emotions as little more than chess pieces.

In a game, sacrifices had to be made. In real life, those sacrifices came with a far steeper price tag.

Finally, she reached a decision. She bit her lip, feeling a jolt of pain which spurred her on towards the door. She pushed it open and hastily moved down the hall, approaching the entrance to the interrogation room. She spotted police officers moving at the end of the hall and spotted another figure shackled to a metal bench. She ignored all of this as best she could, and, inhaling shakily, summoning her nerve, she pushed through the door.

Forester looked up.

In the interrogation room, it smelled of sweat. The air was colder than it had been in the hall. She wondered if this was intentional. In this particular room, she couldn't spot any cameras in the ceiling. She wondered if this was strictly up to code.

She hesitated, lingering in the door.

She thought of Mrs. Washington. Thought of Henry, hanging above his girlfriend, her blood spreading out beneath his feet.

She thought of Cynthia's husband locking himself in his bedroom, unable to face the day.

Artemis had formed many memories with her favorite analysts. She didn't have many friends...

The horrible images from the crime scene were still seared into her mind. Artemis could feel a faint tremor. She shivered and frowned.

Forester raised an eyebrow, leaning back in his chair, casual, comfortable.

How could this be the same man she had seen brutalize three people? Some things just didn't make sense.

"We have the request processing," Artemis said, stiff.

Forester didn't even bat an eye.

He just nodded, as if he knew exactly what she was talking about. The curiosity lingered in his gaze, though.

Maverick and Knuckles shot her uncomfortable looks.

Artemis shook her head. She kept her tone severe. "I wish it hadn't come to this, Mr. Anthony," she said, looking at the younger man.

He shifted uncomfortably, his metal chair sliding across the ground. His handcuffs rattled.

Artemis shivered in the cold interrogation room, prickles rising along her arms.

They needed to provide a reason for Maverick to ignore his uncle's attempts at silencing him.

And Artemis could only think of one person the young man would be more loyal to than his uncle.

She said, "Your father is being transferred."

Forester just nodded, solemn. "They already processed it? I'm impressed. Usually, it takes a couple of days."

Maverick shot a look between them, frowning. "What are you talking about?"

Artemis could still feel the rising sense of uncertainty, but said, enunciating as clearly as she could, "Your father is currently in a maximum-security facility in Naperville. We're transferring him."

Forester rested his hands on the table, nodding. "If you don't play ball with us," Forester said, "we can't play with you."

The young man looked suddenly terrified. "What are you talking about? Knuck, what are they talking about?"

But his uncle was sneering. "They're bluffing. Ignore them. *Lawyer*," he said, insistently.

Artemis, feeling a knot in her stomach, continued and said, "At the new facility, I'm afraid they're a bit overpopulated. Your father is going to have to spend a few months in solitary. I would hate for him to find out that you could've stopped this."

Maverick was staring at her, gaping, mouth unhinged, eyes wide.

"Wait," he said, stammering. "You can't do that."

Artemis shook her head. "We can, and we have. I'm sorry. But if you don't help us, there's nothing I can do."

Forester was nodding still. "She really is a very considerate person," Forester said. "If I were you, I would trust her to help out your old man. But she can't do that, unless you help us."

Knuckles was scowling now. "Mav, don't listen to them. They're full of it."

Forester shrugged. "No skin off my nose," he said. "I don't care if a scumbag spends five months going slowly insane in the dark and the cold. I hear at the new place they only give one meal a day. Pretty awful." Forester was picking at his fingernails and talking as if he were commenting on the weather.

Artemis felt queasy, but also, she felt a daunting sense of inevitability.

"Mav," Knuckles muttered, "keep a lid on—"

"Nah! Screw that," Maverick snapped, turning away from his uncle. "We didn't do anything!" He yelled now, his face gaunt and body shaking. "Nothing!"

Artemis leaned across the table now, frowning at him, using her shadow to create a sort of demarcation between the two men. She didn't even glance at the uncle, as if he wasn't there. Didn't respond to his words, as if she couldn't hear him.

These were all subtle, physical cues. The sort of things that most people ignored. But it was the exact reason that soundtracks in movies or soundscapes in film could conjure all sorts of emotion that the purely visual couldn't. The reason that a properly lit and edited film of even the silliest footage could yield profound results.

It was in the emotion, in the perception.

Half of the human mind was perception. Artemis could remember one of her favorite chess tournaments the previous year. Her opponent at the time had spent nearly an hour in online interviews insulting the fact that he would be facing a woman in an open tournament. He'd had no qualms about suggesting the endeavor was far beneath him.

He'd claimed he'd never played a woman who was a "proper student of the game."

Artemis had taken the words to heart. At first, they'd irritated her, but she knew others were also capable of employing emotional strategies prior to matches—the same way she did.

But in her study and research of the man, she'd determined that simply tossing his comments as sexism wasn't sufficient to understand the man himself. People were often a mixture of motives. And after studying him, she'd reached a course of action.

On the day of the tournament, she'd arrived two hours late to her game *on purpose*. The absence followed by her arrival had thrown her opponent through a loop. The man had prepared so long that sitting there, alone, staring at a board on his own had filled him with a profound sense of both excitement and loneliness.

Then, when she'd arrived, she hadn't said a word. Hadn't looked at him. Hadn't greeted him. She'd moved her pieces quickly, then, slamming them into their places with loud movements, she would hit the clock with equally loud motions.

The combination of being ignored and disrespected had rankled him. She had felt the rising sense of contempt from the man. He'd muttered a few comments like, "typical..." "...as expected..." But he'd been a passive player for most of the tournament. Because she'd irritated him, he went into a line of play that he wasn't prepared for. She showed up two hours late but won in twenty minutes.

She didn't hate the man for his opinions. Didn't even wish him harm. When asked about him after the match, she'd been as gracious as she could manage. But still, in the moment, it had felt good to use his own pride against him.

And all of it came down to the small things. The stage props.

Now, staring at where she leaned forward, swallowing as he met her glare, Maverick shifted uncomfortably in his seat.

Artemis shook her head. "I know what it is to have a father in prison," she said quietly. Even as she spoke, the words surprised her. She wasn't usually willing to go about telling people this.

Maverick stared at her, eyes narrowed. "Bullshit."

She shook her head. "No. Actually, my old man went away when I was about your age." She nodded once.

He snorted at her. "Yeah?" He leered now, leaning forward as well, his chest swelling. "My dad is a killer."

Artemis stared back. "My father murdered seven women, including my sister." She didn't blink, didn't allow even a drop of emotion into her words.

But now Maverick swallowed, looking uncomfortable.

Knuckles was still muttering, but even he had gone quiet now that she'd ignored him. She couldn't see Forester for the moment, as he was behind where she leaned, but this, she decided, was preferable anyway.

"My brother," she said simply, "is a friend of a family. Do you know what that means?"

Maverick let out a long sigh. "I don't care, lady."

"No—no, I guess not. But I've only ever visited my father twice in prison. In fifteen years, I've seen him twice. You want to visit your father, don't you?"

Maverick shook his head, starting to get angry again. Clearly, she'd hit a nerve. "I didn't do *anything*!" he yelled.

"Please," Forester snorted. "You were involved in a burglary that left an older woman with PTSD. She sold her grandmother's house because of you."

"That wasn't proven!" Maverick snapped.

"No?" Forester tapped a finger against the table as if it were a judge's gavel. "What about that girl you harassed at the Napperville mall? That was on camera. You got six months for that."

"Six months of juvie ain't nothing."

Artemis shook her head. "Where were you, Maverick? Where was your uncle?"

Knuckles was just repeating, "Lawyer. Lawyer. Lawyer."

Maverick stared at her. "You... you can't move my dad. That's not right."

"Already done," Forester said. He spoke the lie so seamlessly, as if carrying forth a baton Artemis had passed him. Even as he said it, she felt her stomach twist but didn't take it back. Instead, she said, "Just tell me, Maverick. You can visit your old man tomorrow. Can't you imagine that? Sitting across from him? Hearing him? Seeing him?"

"Things happen in maximum security," Forester said knowingly. "Bad things to bad people—"

"Alright! Shit, you guys are psycho!" Maverick yelled. He had lunged to his feet now. Forester didn't even flinch, remaining where he was, leaning back, the picture of ease.

But now, the younger man was gasping. His uncle tried to say something, but Maverick cut him off with a shout. "We were at *Lil'*

Moriss. It's a bar in the city. We've been there every night for a damn week!"

"Mav," Knuckles said, a growl in his throat. "Shut up."

But his nephew ignored him now, his eyes wide with panic at the thought of his father. The thought of all the things that might never be if he held his tongue. "They've got cameras. They've got witnesses," Maverick yelled. "They'll say. It's in the city anyhow. Two hours from here. We didn't touch Henry."

Artemis leaned back, shooting a quick look towards Forester, accompanying a shrug.

The lanky agent frowned. "You were at this pub every night?"

"Every one," Maverick yelled. "Me and all—no, shut up, Knuck! I don't give a shit!" He yanked his arm from where his uncle was trying to snatch his wrist. "All my uncles were there. We needed neutral ground, yeah? A public place. We were having... having some business talks with—"

"No one!" snapped Knuckles. "We weren't talking with *anyone.*" He'd managed to grab his nephew's arm and yank *hard.*

Maverick yelped as he was pulled back into his seat. The handcuffs shifted and flashed silver where they moved.

As he collapsed in his chair, the thing nearly toppled.

But Artemis was looking at Forester. She didn't care what sort of illicit business the Anthonys had been involved in, visiting Chicago. All she needed to know was if the story checked out, and if it lined up with a timeline the coroner had provided, which meant she would need more access to information that only Forester could provide.

The FBI agent was shaking his head. He looked at Maverick and said, "We're going to check your story."

"Do it!" he yelled. "I'm not lying! We didn't touch Henry! No one did."

Forester studied Maverick for a second, and then reached into his suit pocket. He pulled out a single, white rectangle of a business card. He slid it across the slick table, tapping it with a long finger.

"Give that number a call," he said, looking at the younger man, "if you ever want to do something besides throw your life away. I've got friends out here. Good friends, run good gyms. You're fit. You're young. We could make a fighter of you."

Maverick stared, as if slapped, at the card then up at Forester. He gave a little shake of his head, as if dazed or trying to check to see if he was dreaming.

Knuckles rolled his eyes. Artemis wasn't even sure what to make of the gesture. Forester had done the same thing before once, when back in Seattle. He'd often suggested he had an affinity for the sorts of people in the Anthony family's line of work.

It felt... cliché, almost. Like something out of a bad movie, handing a business card to learn boxing... But on the other hand... there was nothing about Forester that felt cliché. Nothing that made her take his offer as anything less than sincere.

Forester was pushing to his feet now. As he did, though, there was a quiet tap on the door.

Artemis and Forester both turned as the door opened.

A young police officer stood in the hall, wincing and holding up an apologetic hand. In his other hand, he was gripping a phone. He cleared his throat, gesturing with his head for the two agents to approach, which they did.

As they drew nearer, the officer in the door whispered, "Just came in five minutes ago. Thought you should know. There's been another double homicide. This time near the arboretum in Warrenville."

Forester frowned. "What kind of double?"

"A young man hanged. A young woman shot," said the officer, wincing. "It isn't pretty. But... you know, figured it sorta fit with..." he trailed off and waved his hands back towards the table and the Anthonys, who were both muttering at each other under their breath now.

Forester sighed but nodded.

Artemis shot him a look. "So," she whispered, "Do you think Grant would be interested *now*?"

Forester scratched at his head, then shrugged. "She thinks I'm already back in Seattle. Nah. Forget Grant—*I'm* interested. Looks like we're heading back to Warrenville. Checkers, you sure do have a way of attracting serial killers."

Artemis shifted uncomfortably at these words. She followed Forester into the hall. As they moved quickly away from the interrogation room, though, she frowned at this comment.

Not because it had been wrong...

But because it felt *true*.

Something about her family. About her father's legacy... it lingered on her like the odor of a skunk. As if she couldn't quite shake the scent.

She sighed, swallowing and picking up the pace as she hastened alongside Forester, moving quickly down the hall.

"Gotta call that pub on the way," Forester said. "Check their alibis. Why don't you?"

"Me? Why me?"

He shot her a look. "You might not know it yet, Checkers. But you're gonna accept Grant's offer. That's my psychic reading."

"We'll see," she muttered. She didn't add the part where she'd made a bet with herself.

If she was able to solve this case, to prove Henry Rodine's innocence, then Forester could very well be right.

This scared her almost as much as the prospect of visiting a new crime scene.

She hated how it had felt to lie to Maverick just to get information. To manipulate the young man's emotions. To play with his soul.

It left her feeling greasy. Dirty.

Using her father's murders as a point of connection with a killer's son also left her queasy.

Was it worth it?

Was any of this worth it?

She shot a glance towards Forester. He was whistling softly as he strode along, seemingly without a care in the world. She had to move twice as fast just to keep up with his lanky gait.

And as she did, she felt a cold dread settling in her chest.

12

Forester's hand trailed against ferns extending past the trail, brushing against him as he moved down the incline towards the crime scene.

He heard the sound of rushing water, the scent of the stream, heavy on the air, accompanying the fragrance of foliage and flowers.

He shot a look back to spot where Artemis Blythe was moving, slower, accompanying one of the arboretum's staff that had led them to the location. At the bottom of the hill, he spotted police moving about the scene of the crime. For the moment, he hadn't yet noted the bodies.

As Forester moved down the hill, he inhaled slowly, frowning. He shot another look back over his shoulder.

He wasn't usually one given to reading other peoples' emotions. Not because he wasn't perfectly capable of understanding the expression they wore, but because they were often unfamiliar to him. It wasn't *his* language, almost as if he'd studied another tongue just to accommodate his status as a tourist.

He often felt like a tourist among people. Especially those with heightened emotions and stronger feelings.

Artemis Blythe was one such woman.

She was a genius. Analytical, brilliant. That much had been obvious at first. But the more he got to know her, the more it became apparent that lurking underneath it all, there was a strong sense of compassion. A strong sense of hidden pain.

He'd never felt compassion the way others did. Not *really*.

At least... not for anyone else since *her*.

He frowned at the memory, feeling an uncomfortable lance through his chest. He paused, standing with one hand bending a fern leaf back. He held it there, watching the way the branch curved at the stem and loosing a small breath of air.

He *had* felt certain emotions. Strong emotions. Some he'd never thought he'd experience.

But that had all gone away seven years ago, hadn't it?

And somehow... Artemis' father had known about it.

He'd known what Forester had *done* about it.

The tall agent frowned, rubbing at the bridge of his nose. He knew he'd scared Artemis. She wasn't the only one who could read body language. Now, she lingered back, keeping her distance. Clearly scared.

He hadn't *meant* to scare her.

In fact, he'd been trying to protect her.

He knew, firsthand, what happened when one *didn't* protect the people they loved. When one *tried* to lead with things like mercy or compassion.

People died.

He scowled at the memory of her. She'd been... not perfect... no... but...

He sighed, trying not to think too much of her. It had been her fault he'd shown mercy to the man who'd eventually killed her. Had been her pleading with him that had gotten through to his heart.

And in the end, his willingness to listen to her had cost him every damn thing he'd ever cared for.

His hand curled into a fist at his side, and he took a moment to steady himself.

He shook his head. No.

No, far better to forget about that type of thinking. There were benefits to having his chemical make-up. Benefits to living a life without the encumbrances and boundaries outlined by affection or pity or empathy.

He gave another surreptitious glance back towards Artemis.

The way she'd looked at him, though, back in that garage...

The same way his wife had once looked at him. That was why he'd listened to her. Was why he'd shown some semblance of mercy. Wasn't it? He'd allowed his wife's disappointment in him to lead to her own death, and by the time he'd realized what was happening, it was too late.

He rolled his shoulders, wishing—more than anything—Artemis Blythe, the Ghostkiller's daughter, didn't remind him so much of his dead wife.

It hurt being around her.

Hurt in ways that he usually didn't experience pain. But it also hurt in general.

He shook his head, stomping down the trail, kicking dust and reaching the bottom of the hill. Now, his gaze landed on the creek, the water churning past in quick patterns as it fled the slopes and descended towards a bowl in a man-made valley.

The arboretum itself boasted trees from nearly fifty countries. Many of them had been planted over a hundred years ago.

The air was fresh here. The trees spaced perfectly, the groundcover kept trim and tame. But now, as his eyes moved up a particularly large tree with low-hanging branches, he felt his countenance shift. He stared, frowning at the young man hanging from the lowest branch, his feet dangling only a few inches off the ground, the thick rope lashed around the tree.

He spotted where someone from forensics was studying the young man's fingers, shaking his head. "Rope fibers!" the agent called out. "In his fingers."

Forester heard some quiet murmuring. Then the sound of a muttered conference. He glanced over to spot two familiar figures facing the corpse and speaking to each other. They stood a few feet further apart than a private conference might normally entail. One of them was dressed in a neat suit, with perfectly patterned socks and large-rimmed glasses. He looked more like a professor than a detective. He was middle-aged and leaning to speak towards a woman who looked to be at least half his age.

The blonde woman was attractive, something Forester felt no shame in acknowledging, no matter how many times he was hissed at. She had a small notebook in one hand and had been the one to speak first, following the forensic agent's report. She said, "He hanged himself, just like the others."

"Some sort of pact?" asked Detective Ross.

Hardwick nodded. "Must be. Maybe on his phone?"

Ross raised his voice. "Look for the young man's phone, please!"

Other officers, who were already moving around the area or even wading in the stream, searching the bottom of the creek bed, glanced over, nodded and continued their search.

Forester's gaze moved from the poor fellow dangling from the tree, and his eyes landed on the corpse resting amidst tangled roots. A young woman, her dark hair spread around her face like some sort of shawl. Her blood laced into the roots, the crimson stain spilling over the brown, woody humps and pooling amidst the twists and rivulets in the root systems.

Forester frowned, glancing at the young man hanging in the tree, then towards the girl on the ground.

"Anyone find the gun, yet?" Detective Ross called out.

Two officers who were moving about at the base of the tree glanced back. One of them called, "Nothing here—no shell casings either!"

Ross sighed and began to turn to address his partner again, but as he did, his eyes landed on Forester, and he stiffened.

Forester adopted a quick smile. He waved cheerfully.

Ross frowned. Hardwick followed her partner's glare, and she spotted Forester a second later. She also frowned as the tall agent approached.

"Well, isn't it nice to meet again," Forester said, nodding at each of them in turn. He extended a hand to shake, but neither Ross nor Hardwick moved to accept it.

"What are you doing here?" Hardwick said, her voice cold.

"Oh, you know, sight-seeing. Looks like we have another little accident here. Bet you Henry Rodine's ghost did this one."

"We get it," Ross snapped. "It *looks* suspicious. But we have a working theory."

Hardwick nodded, her arm tightening over her notebook.

Forester scratched at his chin. "I see... The suicide-pact theory, huh? Three young men all agree to hang themselves and kill their girlfriends. Is that right?"

Hardwick frowned. "Were you eavesdropping?"

"Yup. Accidentally, though, mostly. Just one quick question."

They just glared at him.

Forester was starting to realize that he elicited this reaction a lot. He also supposed that throat-punching and groin-kicking was off the table in this particular altercation. He adjusted his suit, clearing his throat. "You haven't found any... actual pact, have you? Emails? Phone calls? Scrawled letters? Whispered rumors?"

Neither of the detectives said anything.

"Hmm, I see..." Forester shot a look towards where Artemis lingered at the trailhead, keeping back but glancing around the scene of the crime. She often did this, preferring to get a bird's eye view of things before moving in any closer.

She reached up, brushing her dark hair out of her eyes. As she did the familiar gesture, Forester frowned. He felt another lance of that familiar, emotional pain and turned away, looking at the detectives once more. "Any chance," Forester said slowly, "You're willing to reconsider the serial theory? That Henry Rodine was murdered?"

"What?" said Ross. "By Mr. Bache here?"

Forester glanced back towards the tree. "Was there a connection between Bache and Rodine? What about Martin?"

"Who?"

"The murder-suicide from four months ago. Also, a hanging. Also, a gunshot young woman."

The detectives both looked uncomfortable now. Hardwick, though, cleared her throat and said, "We're looking into every eventuality."

Forester paused, nodding slowly. His intent hadn't been to completely alienate the two detectives. His personality, he'd been told, could not only border on the abrasive but occasionally sally across on raiding missions.

But... still...

He'd learned to play with others over the years. At least, after a fashion.

And working with someone like Desmond Wade had helped. Agent Wade was far more patient than previous partners had been. In fact, Wade had *yet* to ask for a transfer. This, in Forester's record as an agent, was something of a first. He'd already been through five partners.

But one of the things he'd learned working with Wade was how important reciprocation was.

"Look," Forester said simply, "I can offer you what we have if you help us dot some I's. That fair?"

"We don't need any T's crossed," Ross replied. "The FBI isn't involved here. This isn't a serial, and there's been no administrative transfer of jurisdiction. You're out of your depth, Agent Forester."

"What if I told you that we've already interviewed a suspect."

"Oh?" Hardwick said. "Any evidence?" She was using the same tone he'd employed moments before.

Forester hesitated but gave a quick shake of his head. "There's security footage at a pub in Chicago that clears them. We checked on the way here. But my point is, you could use the help. That woman over there is a consultant with us. She's on something of a hot streak in recent weeks."

"We know who Ms. Blythe is," snapped Hardwick. "We don't need the help of a woman who plays games for a living. The experience she has with serials isn't the sort I'd go around bragging about either."

Forester hesitated, studying the woman. She'd clearly meant it as an insult. His brow flickered into a frown as he shot a look towards where Artemis lingered, but then he ran a hand through his hair. "So that's it, huh? Unless I bring the bureau's foot down, you're not going to play nice."

Ross forced a thin-lipped smile, but it didn't reach his eyes. "Perhaps it's best you leave us to our work, hmm?"

Forester turned, deliberately glancing around the crime scene, frowning as he did. The figure hanging from the tree had rope fibers on his fingers. He'd hung the rope himself, then. But no weapon was found...

It seemed clear now, didn't it? Someone had forced the young man to throw the rope then waited for the woman...

Someone was killing young couples, and the detectives were too bull-headed to consider it. He had no doubt that they would eventually come around. In fact, knowing these sorts, they were probably already investigating all eventualities. But participation was off the table.

He sighed to himself, shaking his head and pausing once more to stare at the young woman on the ground. As he passed, he spotted a man in a white jacket opening a wallet he'd pulled from the victim's pocket.

"Hey," Forester said, "let me see that." He didn't hesitate, didn't ask for permission, just extended a hand.

"Wait—Matt, don't give him that!" Hardwick called out from behind him.

But too late, the man in the jacket had already extended the wallet. Forester snagged it. As the man reacted to Hardwick's shout, he hesitated, trying to pull it back, but Forester had already slipped the ID out, holding it between thumb and forefinger.

He studied the name, the information, the address.

Requisitioning the case files through the proper channels would only alert Agent Grant to his whereabouts and create unnecessary friction.

He re-read the name and address of the female victim. A second later, Hardwick's hand shot out, grabbed the ID and snapped it out of his hand.

"Officer Gale," Hardwick was calling, "Would you mind escorting this man from..."

She trailed off as Forester raised his hands in mock surrender and began to march away. After a second, though, he paused and looked Hardwick in the eye.

"You're making a mistake," he said simply.

She glared, making it clear that she didn't care in the least.

Forester frowned back at her, opened his mouth to speak, but then paused at a sudden sound. He glanced over his shoulder towards the road to watch as one of the arboretum gardeners trundled by in a small golf-cart with a wire basket attached to the rear, filled with gardening implements.

He did a double-take, hesitating for the faintest moment. But then, he felt a hand tighten on his arm. He glanced down, looked slowly up, eyes narrowing.

"Don't touch me," he said slowly, his voice fierce.

Detective Ross removed his hand. He said, "Perhaps. I owe you no explanation, Agent Forester, but for the sake of professional courtesy, perhaps you should know..." He cleared his throat, his eyes narrowing behind his glasses. "I have *incontrovertible* evidence that Henry Rodine is a murderer. I know you think we're neglecting the evidence. But I assure you, if you knew what we did, you'd agree."

Forester shifted now, frowning back at Ross. He shrugged once. "What evidence?"

13

Artemis stood on the dirt path, watching the agents interact with Forester. She frowned, refusing to move onto the path, or to look towards the two detectives. From where she stood, though, soft ferns tickling against her ankles, she frowned at the bodies.

A young man was hanging from the tree, the lower branch rising and falling slowly in a mesmerizing oscillation. On the ground, a woman lay amidst the roots, hands splayed, face-down. Dead.

Artemis felt the familiar chill of horror, of grief. The rising sense of outrage at the sheer waste of life.

She thought of her father. How could she not when confronted with such familiar sensations? Artemis' gaze darted along the crime scene, searching for anything that stood out, anything untoward. She frowned as figures moved amidst the underbrush or splashed in the shallows of the stream, eyes to the ground, searching.

Artemis heard the sound of rubber tires crunching against loose earth. She glanced back to see a small golf-cart coasting to a halt on the trail. Tools rattled in a metal cage attached to the back. An arboretum worker, judging by his green shirt with white lettering, hopped out of the front of the golf-cart, clutching two yellow gloves stained with dirt, in one hand.

He was a young man with dark hair and a lip ring. He didn't quite fit the profile of the other gardeners she'd seen as they'd moved slowly through the arboretum. Most of the others had been older, crowned in silver, with wizened skin.

This man was in his twenties, hair jutting to one side like a sort of punk rocker, and besides his lip ring, both his ears were pierced. The man moved down the trail, stepping behind one of the trees and busying himself with a fallen branch, tugging at it.

Artemis watched curiously.

An odd time for the man to choose to fulfill his work obligations. Didn't he see the crime scene? Didn't he see the police?

Didn't he care?

At that moment, her phone buzzed. Artemis glanced down. Cynthia again.

She cursed beneath her breath—in her excitement she'd forgotten to call back. Artemis pulled the phone and answered. "Hello?"

"Artemis!" Cynthia's voice came. "Hello? Are you alright?"

Artemis swallowed. "Fine. Doing fine. We're... we're making progress, Mrs. Washington."

"Okay... Umm... What—what do you know so far?"

Artemis bit her lip. She thought of Henry, Cynthia's husband, locking himself in his room. But what should she say? She didn't know anything conclusive yet. So she said, "We're working on it, ma'am. I... I think we're making good progress."

A sigh. A hesitation. Then... "I wish I could help in some way... But I'm just... just so scared of leaving Henry here alone..." She trailed off and swallowed.

Artemis quickly interjected, "It's fine, Mrs. Washington. I promise you, it's fine. We're handling it. Okay?"

A sigh. "Thank you, Artemis. Truly, from the bottom of my—what was that, dear?" her voice changed in volume and tone. She was speaking to someone else. "Oh... No, just... just the electric company, dear. Alright, I'll make you some soup. I have to go, now," this last line was louder again, back to the phone.

Artemis felt a small jolt of sympathy. "That's fine, Mrs. Washington. I'll see you soon."

"Thank you."

"Happy to help."

"I... thanks..." Cynthia sighed and then hung up, leaving Artemis with an even deeper crater in her soul. She lowered her phone slowly, glancing back towards the young man with the lip ring.

He was far enough away from the crime scene that no one called on him for intruding but close enough now that as he paused, adjusting his grip on his gloves, Artemis noticed him leaning forward a bit, paying a bit *too* much attention towards where Forester was arguing with the detectives.

Artemis stowed her phone, forgetting about the call for a moment as she watched. The young man was frowning where he stood, still listening.

Only now, as she studied him, did she realize his face was pale, as if the blood had drained. His hands were shaking where they gripped the muddy gloves. It almost looked as if he'd recently been crying.

And now he was staring straight at Forester, listening intently.

Artemis, from where she stood, off to the side of the trailhead, hadn't heard Forester's comment, but her attention was fixated by the eavesdropper. He shifted his grip on a small, metal trowel he held in his other hand. The muddy, yellow gloves scraped against the tree as he picked up the large branch. Then, pretending to stretch so he could continue listening to Forester, the young man lingered. He looked up, glancing at some of the police, the forensics agents... and then, his eyes darted to Artemis.

He went still.

She didn't look away.

He suddenly seemed to realize she was staring *right* at him. He swallowed, blinked, pretended as if he was yawning and shot a quick glance over again.

She kept her gaze on him, watching quizzically but openly.

He winced and turned, beginning to hasten back towards his golf cart. Artemis moved as well, walking to intercept. He tried to step out of her way, still carrying the large, fallen branch, but she followed, pushing aside some of the twigs and snapping the edges off as she protected herself from the branches.

She didn't allow him to pass, though, and instead caught his eye. The man shifted nervously, sucking on his lip ring, then shooting a glance over his shoulder. "Sorry, ma'am," he said, clearing his throat and trying to step around again.

Artemis once more blocked his path. "Who are you? Why were you eavesdropping?"

The young man winced, shot her a look, then glanced at the dust again. He exhaled deeply, shifting his grip on his wooden branch and then shook his head. "Umm... John. I work here. I—I wasn't."

"You were," she said. "I saw you."

"N-no," he stammered, keeping his voice low and shooting an uncomfortable glance towards the lingering cops. "No, I did not!" Then, as if realizing she didn't buy it, he mumbled, "Just curious was all. I just got here... late shift," he added as an explanation. "Wanted to see is all. Is it really as bad as they say?"

Artemis looked towards where Forester was still speaking with the two detectives. She said, "Do you know something about what happened here?"

The man was clearly nervous. Uncomfortable. His body language was screaming panic. But Artemis, despite herself, ignored all of this.

She wasn't sure why, but while she could see buttons to push, levers to pull, emotions to play on, she didn't want to do any of it. In a way, it felt like penance for how she had maneuvered in the last interrogation. Besides, watching the young man, he seemed shy, uncomfortable. Not dangerous.

And so, she kept her tone calm but gentle. Artemis could remember the first woman to ever hug her. Mrs. Kramer. The first home where Artemis had ever felt affection, compassion, had been the Kramer household. It was strange to think, but not all of her memories from Pinelake were miserable. Not all of them were so bad.

In fact, now, standing in another state, she almost felt strangely nostalgic. It was the scent of the water, the vegetation, the thick foliage. Even some of the trees looked familiar. No mountains, though. Illinois was too flat for that. But still, it all reminded her of home.

Channeling her inner Mrs. Kramer, Artemis said, softly, "You're safe. You don't have to talk to the police if you don't want to. What caught your attention? Was it one of those detectives?"

The young man adjusted his grip on the two yellow, mud-covered gloves. He swallowed, his pronounced Adam's apple bobbing, but then, in a low, shaky voice, he said, "I think I made a mistake; I was just curious. That's all."

He tried to force a smile and a quick nod.

Artemis studied him now, piecing together what information she could.

She had already asked if he was interested in the detectives. Clearly, that wasn't the answer. But sometimes, given enough of a pause, one could pretend omniscience by repeating a separate question with equal conviction. Right now, she was fishing.

But she had some clues. Especially given the young man's age. She had also asked if he knew anything about the case. He hadn't reacted in guilt. He was scared; not because of some type of remorse, and she didn't get the sense, looking at him, that she needed to strong-arm him.

She said, clearly, "You're involved."

No reaction. Not even a twitch. Just discomfort. As if he had barely heard her.

And so, with equal conviction, reaching out now and gripping his arm, she said, just as firmly, just as confidently, "You know someone who is involved."

Now he tensed. The muscles on his wrist went taut beneath her fingers.

He looked her in the eyes. He shook his head. His voice rose in pitch. "It's *not* like that!" He yanked his arm back. "Sh-she didn't hurt anyone. She was nearly killed. Just, she's a friend. I don't want to drag her into this again."

"Again?" Artemis said.

But the young man tightened his grip on the two gloves. He said, "I don't know anything. Leave me alone!"

He turned and began to move towards the small golf cart laden with gardening tools.

Artemis nearly called out after him; she could have stopped him. She could have told Forester. She could have even asked one of the detectives to detain him. And yet, she didn't say a word. She just watched the young man with the dark hair walk away. In a way, he almost reminded her of her brother.

She wasn't an FBI agent. This wasn't what she had trained to be. She played a game for a living. All of this was too much. She was in over her head.

She sighed faintly, closing her eyes, and when she opened them again, the small golf cart was trundling away, fast, hastening up the hill and disappearing from sight.

Someone else was involved but as a *victim*... In a way, he had given her enough puzzle pieces to make sense of it.

Artemis swallowed slowly and then turned, her lips sealed now. She didn't want to stop the young man. She wouldn't strong-arm anyone else. Not today. Hopefully never again.

She was starting to regret the vow she had made to herself; did she really want to join with Agent Grant, to put herself through months of training, working as a consultant on the side, to what? Feel like this forever? Caught between impossible choices, with no clear answer and no good result?

She scowled, feeling a sudden spurt of contempt.

Pity kills the mind. Another one of Helen's admonishments.

Artemis had to be smarter. She had to figure it out. She could outthink this. She knew she could.

It was dangerous ground to place her trust in her own mental abilities. But who else was there to trust?

Forester? He was a loose cannon.

The detectives? They clearly didn't believe her.

Agent Grant? The woman was using the situation as a recruitment tool.

No. Artemis had to solve this on her own. She looked towards Forester, waiting until she caught his eye. He raised an eyebrow at her, and then, she gestured at him.

The young man had given her an idea. She wasn't sure if it would yield fruit. But, for the moment, they had nothing else to go on. It couldn't hurt to take a shot in the dark.

14

Artemis shot a look towards where Forester settled in the front seat of the vehicle, waving a hand in irritation to swipe a mosquito buzzing near his ear. He slammed the front door, under the darkening sky, then turned to look directly at her.

"Well, *shit*," he said.

She blinked. "Umm, sorry?"

He sighed, shaking his head and frowning. "Checkers..." he trailed off, glancing through the windshield now, wearing a scowl.

"What is it?" she said.

He inhaled, clearly lost in thought, but then he glanced back and shook his head. He put the car in gear and began to back out of the parking lot of the arboretum, moving away from the backdrop of verdure.

Artemis hesitated, frowning. "Did the detectives say something? Henry's dead. They can't possibly suspect that he had something to do with this."

"They... they found something," Forester said slowly. "A video clip online. It's been seen by hundreds of people. A lot of the comments..." He shook his head, wincing. "A lot of the comments are of others egging him on, encouraging him. The detectives think Henry started something when he posted the video. Spread the idea to others."

"What idea?"

Instead of replying, Forester reached into his suit pocket, pulled out his phone, swiped up on the screen and extended it towards her with a little wiggle of his hand.

She hesitated, but then slowly accepted the device, frowning as she did.

Forester said, "Just... I respect that he's your friend's grandkid. But that doesn't look good."

Artemis frowned and lifted the phone. The screen was black with a small, white triangle in the center. She clicked the play button and watched. The speakers crackled from poor audio quality, but then after a few seconds, the image became clearer.

She saw a young man with strong features like his grandfather, and the smiling eyes of his mother, appear on screen, grinning, his teeth flashing. It took a second for her mind to make the connection that she was watching the video of a dead man.

And while Henry Rodine had his mother's eyes, the smile he directed wasn't a very pleasant one. All leer, all contempt.

Artemis watched as the blurry image came further into focus. Henry was grinning as he spoke into the camera.

"Damn," he said, chuckling and waving something in his left hand. "Man... kid like that? Only know one thing. That's right... You want to mess with me? With me?" he widened his eyes, staring into the camera. And then leaned back again, chuckling. Only now did Artemis realize the glinting, swaying item in his hand was a gun.

She frowned. Henry continued to wave the weapon, pointing it one way then the other. "Pop, pop," he said. "That's how it's gonna go if he keeps lipping off. Look at him—I mean just *look*." Artemis frowned, leaning in as the video footage shifted.

Now, Henry was pointing the camera between two metal seats. It took her a second to realize that the young man was standing under bleachers. And there, illuminated by bright lights, she spotted a football field with figures running about. A second later, there was a burst of cheering, a scatter of applause and some shadowy movement as legs in the stands shifted.

But Henry didn't seem to care about the sport. Instead, he was pointing his camera towards a single figure, sitting on a bench, arms wrapped around himself. The figure didn't notice Rodine and his gun in the shadows beneath the bleachers. Didn't notice the camera.

The figure was round, his plumber's crack showing through the gap in the stadium seating. Henry was chuckling quietly as he pointed the camera.

Artemis couldn't quite make out the person in question. Half of him was obscured by the stadium seating. He wasn't cheering as much as the others, though.

In fact, he sat uncomfortably, his arms crossed. He let out a little sigh, his long bangs rising and falling.

Henry pointed the gun towards the stands, raising it and aiming towards the young man sitting there. He then whispered in the speaker, "*Bang, bang.*" He broke into giggling, and then the video feed died.

Artemis stared at the screen in equal parts confusion and horror. She glanced up at Forester. "I... I mean... when was this posted?"

Forester tapped a finger against the screen as they began to move slowly down the long trail towards the exit to the arboretum.

She read the description beneath the video. "Hang on," she said suddenly. "This was posted five months ago!"

Forester nodded. "Five months, yeah. But do you know who that kid is?"

Artemis said, "The one in the stands?"

"Yeah. His name is Kyler Martin. He and his girlfriend were the first two victims," Forester said simply. "The ones from four months ago. And look at the comments."

Artemis scrolled down, frowning as she did, reading the black text against the white background. She felt her stomach twist.

The text comments beneath the video were even worse than the movie itself, which was saying something. Many of them were attacking the appearance of the teenager in the stands. Others were giving advice on how Henry ought to take his revenge. Some were calling for him to hurt the young man. Others mentioned worse violence. A few, she noticed, suggesting 'hanging.'

She scowled, shaking her head. "What is this?" she murmured.

"According to Ross," Forester replied, "They got that video from one of Henry's classmates. By the sound of things, Kyler Martin and Henry got into an argument in class. Kyler insulted Henry, and Henry threatened to make him pay. The video was taken about a week after the incident."

Forester gave a curt shake of his head as he pulled out of the arboretum drive and moved back onto the main street. "He posted this one month before Kyler and his girlfriend were killed."

Artemis let out a little sigh, reaching up and lightly touching either side of her forehead with her fingers. "Do you think I should..." She trailed off and went quiet, lost momentarily in her own thoughts.

Was this something she ought to tell Mrs. Washington?

Clearly, Henry wasn't as rehabilitated as she'd been led to believe. She glanced towards Forester's phone again. "So what's the working theory, then? They think Henry killed Kyler? And then someone retaliated?" She waved a hand over her shoulder. "That doesn't explain what we just saw back there."

Forester shook his head. "I got the girl's name who was shot at the arboretum. Lucy Kent."

"Do we know if she's connected to either victim?" Artemis said, frowning.

Forester gave a quick shake. "Not yet. I haven't had a chance to really look into it, though."

Artemis sighed. She didn't know what to make of the disturbing video footage. Rodine was clearly threatening the young man. Some of the comments on the video had been hair-curling. She murmured, "Any chance someone who saw this video might have been following what happened to Kyler? And then Henry?"

Forester sighed. "I was thinking I might send the comments to Wade to see if he can get a list of IP address that are local. Not sure if he's going to want to do that, though."

Artemis frowned. "I see. Well... It's worth a shot at least."

Forester nodded. "All I'm saying is we might not be able to think of Henry as the victim here. At least... not the only victim. Something else is going on. There's a chance he killed Kyler. A good chance."

"But he was hanged *before* his girlfriend, Paige, was shot. He didn't kill Paige."

"No... No, I guess not. But that doesn't clear him of—"

"I know!" Artemis closed her eyes briefly, inhaling. "I know," she repeated in a quieter voice.

Artemis focused, trying her best to arrange her thoughts, placing them properly. She exhaled slowly as her mind spun, and then she said,

"I think looking into those internet commentators makes sense. But I have a lead of my own."

Forester shot her a curious glance. She nodded slowly. "I was approached while at the arboretum," she said simply. "A young man. He was... well, it's not important. I don't think he's involved, but I think he knows someone who is."

Forester looked away from the road now, his bedraggled hair fluttering from the wind through the open window. "Hang on, what?"

She said, firmly, "I think we need to look deeper. Into any other cases that are similar to this one. Involving young women." She thought of what John had said back by the crime scene. How he'd been intent on protecting his female friend. She nodded more adamantly now. "I think... I think I need your help Forester—I don't have access to case files or information like you do."

Cameron studied her. But then he nodded a single time. Instead of making some quip or comment, he returned his attention to the road, picking up speed. Usually, Forester would keep well within the speed limit, preferring to travel at his own pace, but now, he increased in speed. Faster... faster... *faster* still.

She exhaled shakily, feeling a cold tremor along her back.

The help of the FBI database would have to be the edge she needed. Already, three young couples had been killed. Henry Rodine wasn't the reformed young man she'd been led to believe, not that she thought Mrs. Washington had intentionally misled her.

And by the looks of things, whoever, whatever individual or group, was behind these murders wasn't done yet.

She shot a glance into the rearview mirror, peering in the direction of the arboretum. The large, green foliage poking out above the encircling fence.

She sighed, returning her attention to the road as Forester hastened back towards their hotel.

"So you met a witness back there?" Forester interrupted her trail of thoughts, his voice quiet. "And you didn't mention anything? Did you get a name? An address?"

Artemis bit her lower lip. But she simply shook her head. "Forget about him," she said.

Part of her remembered when she'd been a teenager. Dragged into a police station for a crime she had nothing to do with. Because someone she'd grown up loving had made horrific choices.

In the short term, yes, forcing the young man through scare tactics to provide more information was an effective strategy.

But long term? He'd resent the police. Resent their methods.

Artemis fidgeted uncomfortably as she thought this.

That wasn't why... why *she* was giving grief to the police, was it? That wasn't the core behind her aversion to Agent Grant's proposal... *was it*?

Regardless, it felt cathartic to think that she was doing for John what no one had ever done for her or Tommy.

And in Tommy's case, he hadn't just gone off the rails, he'd dove off a damn cliff.

No... No, she'd solve this without traumatizing another young man. She still couldn't shake the look of horror in Maverick's eyes. Couldn't shake the feeling of how easy it had been to lie to the young man. To bluff. To use deception and manipulation to get her way.

She shook her head, quietly vowing to herself one thing...

If this all turned out how she hoped. If she was able to solve this case...

She wouldn't do it *that* way again. No matter what. She refused to use her mind, to use her training, her upbringing, as a cudgel to beat others into submission.

It made her feel...

Too much like *him*.

Some people said the road to hell was paved with good intentions. But in her opinion, the road wasn't paved at all, and truly good intentions were an off-ramp. A buffer against her lesser nature.

She settled in, staring through the window. Even as the skies darkened, she felt a gloom spread across the horizon.

With Forester's help, she'd finally have the information that only law enforcement could access. She'd finally be able to make some actual progress on this case.

15

Artemis sat on the floor in her hotel room while Forester reclined at the small kitchen table, peering at his laptop. Artemis had her own computer open, feeling the warmth of the base press against her legs. She waited patiently as Forester muttered to himself, clicked something, then said, "There you are... that's the file."

She watched as an email showed up in her inbox; with a quick Tab-click, she opened a new window, and her eyes were already moving, reading the file he'd sent.

He winced sheepishly and said, "Might be best, you know, you don't *tell* anyone I sent you that. As for the content, I've compiled what we have on the three cases in one folder." Forester added briskly, "Technically, I'm not supposed to back door the precinct's case files, but as you might imagine, our friendly detectives haven't exactly been forthcoming with coroner reports or crime scene photos." Forester shook his head and frowned at his computer. "Thankfully," he murmured, "Desmond is a bit of a computer nerd."

Artemis glanced over. She hadn't pegged Forester's partner, Agent Wade, the ex-Green Beret who was built something like an action figure, for being into computers. This only made her like Wade a bit more.

She returned her attention to the file Forester had sent then began to read.

As she scrolled through the case files, studying the information, she tapped her fingers against her keyboard, listening to the keys rattle "The crime scene photos from the historic house are the same as I remember," Artemis said softly. "Did Detective Ross give you access?"

Forester waved his hand. "Let's just say inter-departmental cooperation is a one-way street where the Bureau is concerned. Once you have an inroad to the connected database, there are options."

Artemis frowned at him. "You mean you had someone get this illegally?"

Forester shook his head. "It's not illegal. I..." He cleared his throat importantly. "—requisitioned it in a somewhat unusual fashion."

Artemis shook her head and returned her attention to the high-resolution photos of the crime scene. She moved back to the case from four months ago, the one Forester had found in the article online.

Now, staring at full-resolution photos of the victims, she felt the same, sinking sensation in her stomach, especially because she recognized the face of the man who had been hanged.

The same face she had seen in Henry's taunting, threatening video.

So far, the girlfriends hadn't been connected to the videos. Their names hadn't come up in any search. Artemis paused, considering this. "Kyler Martin and Hannah Lee were the first victims," she said.

Forester nodded, frowning at her.

She continued, "Henry Rodine and Paige Deroza were killed next. Then Lucy Kent and..." She glanced at the final file. "Matthieu

Bache." She paused, shivering as she remembered the young man's corpse dangling from the arboretum tree above the stream.

Here, though, Forester looked up sharply. "Hang on, what?"

She glanced over. "Matthieu Bache," she said. "The victim we just saw. His name is in this file." She tapped her computer screen then winced, quickly wiping the smudge with her sleeve.

Forester, though, was frowning, staring at his computer. "M. Bache," he said slowly. "Huh."

"What is it?"

Forester cleared his throat. "I've been getting the IP address back on the comments beneath Henry's video..." He massaged his eyes. "It's so many damn names." He let out a long breath but steadied himself. "But so far, I recognize two of them."

Artemis winced. "Let me guess," she murmured. "Henry Rodine and Matthieu Bache?"

"No, actually."

She stared.

"Henry *took* the video but no comments. However, Kyler commented on the video. He was using an alias, but he makes a comment at the bottom of the page. Just a frowning face and a few middle-finger emojis..."

Artemis tilted her head. "So these guys all knew each other. Matthieu was connected to Henry and his video threatening Kyler."

"Looks like it... Think that's our connection?"

Artemis paused but then said, "Kyler was the *first* victim, though. So why were Henry and Matthieu killed later?"

Artemis returned her attention to her computer.

As she scrolled down the most recent case file, towards the scant text where it had quickly been ruled another murder-suicide, she said, "What if we're looking at this wrong?"

Forester replied, "In what way?"

"What if this wasn't about the young men at all? What if the girls were the real targets? What if the killer is hunting women out of jealousy or some twisted urge?"

"Well... we can already tell he is pretty twisted."

Artemis frowned at the pictures, doubling back and looking at the womens' names. She murmured quietly, "They were all just out of high school, do you think that has something to do with it? Maybe we should be looking at teachers. Coaches. Instructors. School guidance counselors."

"Did the victims attend the *same* school?"

Artemis scrolled through the information again, and it took her a while. She didn't know quite where to look. Forester, though, said, "Check the tab on personal info." And then, before she could, he said, "No, looks like they went to different schools. Except for Henry and Kyler. But all the girls and Matthieu were from different schools."

Artemis hesitated and looked up, frowning at Forester. "They both went to Naperville Northwest. Do you think there's a way we can search recent cases by keyword?"

Forester lowered the lid of his laptop a couple of inches, raising an eyebrow at her. "What are you thinking?"

"I'm curious if maybe we can find anyone else related to that school who was involved in a violent crime."

"You're still considering that mysterious witness of yours at the arboretum"

"He mentioned there was a young woman connected to the case. A previous victim." Artemis trailed off then said, "You know how people get when they talk about those they're fond of."

Forester shook his head. But said, "Alright, so we want to look up young women who attended Naperville Northwest, who were involved in a violent crime as the victim. Is that right?"

Artemis winced. "Possibly?"

"Keyword searches work. Here, give me a second."

Forester turned his attention to the computer again, tilting it back with his fist.

She waited nervously, watching as he typed away.

And then, after a few moments, he said, "We have quite a few bomb threats, gun threats, but most of them look as if they were deemed fake."

"I feel like we're looking for something more substantive than that. Something that affected individuals. Students."

Forester made a grunting sound that caught somewhere in his throat. But then his eyebrows went up. "Actually, there's been more than one fistfight at the school. Though, I'm thinking you don't mean that. I have a stabbing."

"A stabbing? When was that?"

"About three years ago. Since then, they've installed metal detectors."

Artemis paused. "Any of the names familiar?"

Forester hesitated but then shook his head. "The victim was an adult. A coach on one of the wrestling teams."

"Huh. Maybe not, then. Anything else?"

Forester continued to scroll but was now shaking his head. "A lot of small things. No murders. No attempted murders. I don't see any reports about that video of Henry's, which means the detectives were right in that no one came forward with it."

Artemis put her computer to the side and began to get to her feet. But as she approached, Forester suddenly said, "Hang on, what about this?"

She continued to move around the table, but her eyes were now fixed on the tall agent.

He said, "It looks like we have another hanging."

"Wait, what?" A slow prickle spread along her skin.

Forester nodded quickly. "A student at Northwest hanged himself in the gym. From the basketball hoop."

Artemis just stared.

"But hang on, no," Forester said quickly. "It was a suicide."

"That's the theory for these other cases. But what if—"

Forester said, "His own parents said it was a suicide."

Artemis leaned back, exhaling. "How could they know for sure? What was the student's name?"

"Jamar Young. By the looks of things, he had told his school counselor he was thinking of killing himself. In fact, I don't see the file here, but apparently he left a video message to his parents saying he was going to do it." Forester's eyes darted back and forth as he studied the screen. He looked up, regarding Artemis where she lingered by the table.

Artemis let out a long sigh. "When was this?"

"About two years ago."

"Do we have an address for his parents? For anyone who might've known him?"

Forester, though, was now clicking on small symbols of miniature paperclips. He hesitated then said. "Huh... look here."

Artemis leaned in, studying the screen.

"An addendum was added to the report," Forester said slowly. "Looks like one of the witnesses... hmm... A cousin who was living with the family at the time... She didn't think it was suicide. She believed someone murdered her cousin."

Artemis leaned in as well, reading the hastily jotted note on the screen, which had then been scanned and uploaded in blurry resolution, as if the information itself was mostly throwaway and nothing much worth considering.

"The cousin," Artemis said slowly. "Does she still live with the family?"

Forester glanced at the file, then, murmuring the name written in the top left for witness information, he said softly, "Sofia Perez... I'll check the DMV." After a flurry of his scarred and calloused fingers flying over the keys, he nodded and leaned back. "Huh. Yeah, looks like she still lives with the family."

Artemis shook her head. "And she felt that it *wasn't* a suicide? A murder? But only one victim, right?"

"Yup. Just the one... Maybe the killer started with one then began escalating? You think maybe Kyler here was our killer's first victim?"

"It can't be Henry," Artemis said.

"Never said it was."

"But you were thinking it."

"No; I just watched that same video you did, though, didn't I?"

Artemis bit her lip. She wanted to protest but found she couldn't do much in that moment but nod slowly. She'd seen the troubling video too. She wasn't sure what to think of Henry Rodine. If she had seen that video *before* speaking with Mrs. Washington, she wasn't sure *what* she might have thought.

Still, *someone* had killed the two most recent victims *after* Henry had already died. Someone else out there had killed Henry... unless... unless he really had committed suicide?

She shook her head, frowning.

No... no, it made the most sense that someone else was committing the murders. No blood on the back of the chair at the scene with Henry meant his girlfriend had died *after*. Someone else had killed him. And that same someone had killed Matthieu and Lucy at the arboretum.

But if Henry wasn't involved... why had Henry sent that video, taunting Kyler? And then the very next month, Kyler and his girl-friend had ended up dead.

Artemis massaged her eyes. "We need to speak with Sofia Perez," she said slowly. "The cousin of that guy who hanged himself at the gym."

"You think maybe she knows something?"

"I mean... look at the report. The officer even used it as a coaster for his coffee."

Forester traced the brown ring on the scan of the white paper. He ended by tapping his finger in the center of the circle. "Yeah... just the claim made. No evidence. Alright... The parents thought he'd committed suicide, but what if Sofia was right?"

Artemis nodded. "What if her cousin was *also* murdered two years ago? Maybe that was the real first victim of our killer."

"Let's go speak with Ms. Perez."

Artemis was also thinking something else. The young man at the arboretum had been worried that a young woman he knew would be connected to the case and potentially be put in harm's way if he brought her name up.

Now Artemis was beginning to wonder if maybe Sofia was the woman in question...

She must have been close to Jamar Young before he'd died.

But why did she believe it was a murder while the rest of the family suggested it was suicide?

Artemis frowned, adjusting her sweater as Forester pushed to his feet, slammed his laptop closed and moved towards the hotel door.

As they hastened forward, Artemis' phone buzzed.

She glanced down, hesitant. "Oh," she murmured, frowning. "H uh..."

"What is it?" Forester said, standing by the door, having already pushed it halfway open.

Artemis waved away the question. "Umm... n-nothing," she said quickly. "Just..." She frowned, reading the text from Jamie.

You should take it.

A simple, straightforward response.

You should take it. The job... he wanted her to take the job in Seattle.

She found herself smiling despite her best efforts to hold back the expression.

Forester tried to peer over her shoulder at her phone, leaning in. She stepped back, hastily pocketing her device. "Hey," she said, "rude." She frowned at him.

Forester held up his hands quickly, flashing a quick, schoolboy grin. "Just curious what's got you smirking like that."

She maintained her frown. "I don't see how that's your business."

To her surprise, Forester nodded once and shrugged a single shoulder.

"Yeah... yeah, you're right. Sorry," he said quickly, placing a hand over his heart.

She frowned at him. "You know, I never can tell if you're teasing or being sincere."

"And that," he said, nodding and then turning on his heel, "is all a part of my charm. It's getting late, Checkers. You sure you wanna do this tonight?"

"Better tonight than tomorrow," Artemis said, feeling some of her giddiness fading as the text message from her childhood sweetheart was forgotten and her attention was once again refocused on the case. "If Ms. Perez really does know something about Mr. Young's death... it could be the clue we need."

Forester shrugged both shoulders this time and picked up the pace, moving around a banister and taking the stairs two at a time.

As Artemis followed, she shot a quick look to make sure she'd remembered to shut her hotel room door. Once this was determined, her hand tapped against her pocket, feeling where her phone protruded. Her fingers traced the outline, and she allowed her mind to wander, if only briefly.

Jamie Kramer wanted her to return to the Pacific Northwest... Seattle? Or even her hometown?

The Kramer household was the first place she'd experienced... *warmth* in a home.

Now, all of that had ended too, though.

She sighed shakily. Mr. Kramer had visited her father in prison. Somehow, her old man managed to contaminate everything he touched.

Everyone he interacted with.

There were multiple reasons to return to Pinelake. But she'd already made a commitment. Either she solved this case... or she didn't.

A lot hung in the balance.

And now, the question was clear...

Had Mr. Young really committed suicide, or had he been murdered?

And if so, how was this killer striking without leaving physical evidence? Each new piece of evidence was just a breadcrumb along the trail.

But where did the trail lead?

Artemis desperately hoped she could find out before two more victims were claimed.

16

The car doors slammed, the lights flashed, and Artemis wrapped her arms around her thin form, wincing against the chill in the air. Her dark hair fluttered across her cheeks, and she paused to brush her hair behind one ear, blinking up at the flashing porchlight from the left side of the duplex.

Forester moved behind her, glancing from his phone to the address above the black, slotted mailbox.

"This is it," he said, rubbing his hand against his pantleg. "You want me to do the talking or you?" He shot her a look.

She shifted uncomfortably. It almost felt as if she were being tested. She cleared her throat, feeling her anxiety return and swirling in her stomach, but then she nodded and took two quick steps up the wooden stairs, avoiding a particularly moldered section of the bottom step.

As she reached the glass patio door, she nearly turned and retreated.

Her anxiety was spiking, and she let out a few deep breaths. She paused, hand raised, but then closed her eyes, feeling a jolt of tangible anxiety through her gut.

She glimpsed Forester watching her in the reflection of the glass, a frown on his face. She closed her eyes again, trying to inhale shakily.

But once more, the thought of approaching an unknown family in order to interview a live-in cousin about their recently dead family member wasn't exactly an easy conversation.

She inhaled again and tried to calm her rapidly pounding heart.

She heard shuffling behind her and glanced in the reflective glass of the patio door to see Forester standing at the base of the stairs. He said, quietly, his voice low, "It's going to be alright. You're going to do just fine. I can speak with them if you'd like."

He spoke soothingly, slowly. She noticed he was tapping his right hand against the rail of the steps.

Tap. Tap.

He was doing it so loudly, she felt nearly certain it would hurt his finger. But he didn't stop, continuing the clear, repetitive motion.

Tap. Tap. Tap.

This, she knew, was sometimes prescribed for people struggling with a panic attack. A single motion or loud noise or focusing question could help redirect a mind.

Artemis tried to focus on the rapid tapping. While the physical ramifications of her panic attacks settled in her stomach, they originated in her mind. One of the disadvantages of having a mind like hers, capable of processing quickly and tracking branching patterns in a matter of split seconds, was how often that same mind, used as a tool, could be turned against her and weaponized.

For Artemis, she took a shaky step forward, bracing against the banister, inhaling, exhaling, her eyes closed.

She could feel her emotions threatening to spill over. Could feel the heightening of her fear, anxiety, sadness. Forester was no longer talking but stood nearby, still tapping his finger.

He didn't offer to take the lead from her a second time.

She wondered why this was.

At any moment, she could take him up on his offer. She could step down and allow Forester himself to lead. He was the FBI agent after all. He was the one with the badge and the gun and the bona fides.

Even as she considered it, she felt a sour taste in her mouth. She didn't want to concede.

Didn't want the anxiety to win out.

And so, summoning stiff resolve and courage, willing it, she stood a bit straighter. This was the extent of the effect of courage.

And yet, now, focusing on her breathing, on Forester's tapping finger, she finally relaxed enough to exhale. To hold her breath. Inhale, hold.

And then, with a swallow, she reached out and pushed the doorbell. It rang.

The bright light above the porch served as something of a spotlight, illuminating Artemis and Forester where they stood.

Forester was no longer tapping his finger.

He had once said his mother used to have panic attacks. Sometimes, it almost felt like Forester treated her differently when she started to panic. As if he saw someone *else*.

She shook her head, slowly, trying to relax.

And then, she heard the sound of the door opening inside the patio. A few moments and then a woman in a bathrobe, with hair curlers in a mess of brown and gray hair, reached the door and pushed the glass open, leaving smudged fingerprints on the surface.

She peered out into the dark, blinking a few times and wincing, as if adjusting to the bright beam from the light above the door.

The woman smoothed her blue, cotton bathrobe, reaching down to adjust the sash. "Hello?" she said cautiously, glancing between the two of them with confusion, but then a rising suspicion became apparent in the way she took a half step back and attempted to close the door a bit.

Neither Artemis nor Forester moved to intercept.

Forester remained where he stood on the ground, at the base of the stairs. Artemis, on the top step, lowered her hands and shifted restlessly.

Again, facing the woman, Artemis felt a strange sense of anxiety rising within her.

But after a few quick exhales, she said, "Apologies, Mrs. Young. We're here to speak with your niece, Ms. Perez."

The woman in the door frowned. "Sofia? What do you want with her?"

Artemis struggled to think what she ought to say next. It was so strange for her mind to go blank. She shifted, willing thoughts to catch up; after a few moments, she remembered why she was there. "Apologies," she said. "We, or, I should say *he* is with the FBI. I consult." As she said it, she shot a look towards Forester; he didn't correct her.

"The FBI?" She sounded a lot colder all of a sudden. "What is this about?"

Artemis balked at the sudden change in the woman's tone; she hesitated, glancing back towards Forester. The agent didn't remove his ID, though. Either thinking it was unnecessary, as it hadn't been questioned, or worried it might just trigger the woman.

Now, Artemis sighed, exhaling deeply and closing her eyes. She said, quietly, "We have a couple of questions, ma'am..."

"Is this about…" The woman paused, caught herself, swallowed and stared at the ground suddenly. She hesitated then looked up again, her eyes carrying a haunted quality. "What *is* this about?" she said more firmly now. "Ever since my niece moved here, I've been her caretaker, so if you want to speak to her, tell me what you want."

Artemis said, quietly, "We need to ask her about some comments she made…" She paused, trying to think of the best way to phrase it without offending the older woman. But then she shook her head and tried again. "We need to clear up something from a police report. It's probably nothing… but is she home?"

Mrs. Young stood in the door, shifting in her bare feet, her long, fuzzy bathrobe swaying with the motion. In the end, she gave a quick tug at her sash and then said, her tone carrying every hint of acerbity, "If I get even a whiff you're harassing my niece, then I'll sue each of you individually. Sofia has been through enough! We all have!"

And with that and a final flourish of her robe, the woman marched away, moving back into the house and disappearing from sight.

Artemis stared at the closing door and winced. Her stomach was still churning horribly. Forester, though, gave her a pat on the shoulder. "You did fine," he said. "Good job. Any thought to how you want to approach this with the girl?"

Artemis sighed, looking back at Forester. She thought of what the young man in the arboretum had said. He'd known a girl affected by the case. He'd seemed stunned at spotting someone hanging in the arboretum. She would have to confirm that the arboretum worker had been speaking about Sofia, but she was confident at this point that she was right.

Artemis gave a quick nod towards Forester, but before she could reply, the door to the house opened again. A young woman with dark hair and two stud earrings was standing in the door—both earrings were in her left ear. She glanced at the two agents, nervously, hesitating where she stood in the doorframe.

The aunt could be seen just past her, watching all of them with eyes like a hawk, scowling whenever her gaze landed on Artemis or Forester.

"I'll keep the door open," she said firmly. Then she gave an affectionate squeeze on Sofia's shoulder. "Call if you need me. I'm just inside."

Ms. Perez nodded once, tucking her hands inside her pockets and taking a tentative step onto the porch. Through the half-open screen door, propped by Artemis' foot, she said, "W-would it be okay if we stay on the porch?" she said. "I-I'm n-not comfortable in..." She swallowed, staring down the steps at the street, her eyes lingering on their car then moving back to the agents. She winced and gave a little, apologetic shake of her head.

"Of course," Artemis said quickly. "We can chat here. Would you like to take a seat?" She waved a hand towards some wicker chairs circling a tiny, glass table with a pot of plastic flowers.

Forester remained standing at the bottom step. Artemis looked at him, feeling a flash of panic, but he gave a small, encouraging nod, maintaining his posture at the base of the stairs.

Artemis could feel her heart pounding wildly now. She wasn't sure what Forester was even thinking—she couldn't interrogate someone on her own... She *wasn't the agent.*

Then again, she was the one considering training, wasn't she?

In a way, this was almost like a preliminary step.

Artemis tried to exhale deeply enough to dislodge at least some of her nerves and then she stepped through the open door, smiling politely as the door swung slowly shut behind her. Forester didn't remain where he was, nor did he watch through the glass. Instead, the agent turned and—with long strides—moved back towards the hood of the car.

He reached out with his scarred hand to brace against the front of the vehicle before lowering onto the hood, using it as a bench and crossing his legs as he stared across the street in the opposite direction, leaving Artemis and Sofia to their privacy.

The door to the house was still open, like one giant ear pressed to the patio, but this fear of being overheard wasn't the reason she felt suddenly tongue-tied. Rather, as she faced Sofia Perez, and lowered slowly into one of the wicker chairs, she could feel just how out of her depth she was.

In a way, it almost felt like a match. But there was no chess board, and Perez wasn't an opponent.

She was a witness to something... horrible. Something she'd reported to the police, but that they'd never taken seriously.

And so, Artemis said, quietly, "Ms. Perez, my name is Artemis Blythe. It's good to meet you."

Sofia was shifting nervously. As she adjusted her seat, Artemis couldn't help but notice the way she shifted it back in the direction of the open house door. Artemis knew from experience and interacting with others that sometimes trauma could make it difficult for certain types of people to leave their houses.

Now Sofia looked how Artemis had felt only moments before. She even had a small dappling of sweat across her forehead, which she wiped with the back of her sweater sleeve, her fingers trembling. She said, "Th-thank y-you." She paused, frustrated with herself, inhaling slowly, trying to calm, then said again, "Th-thank... d-d-damn it." She winced at the stutter. Paused; then, closing her eyes, said, "S-sorry. I... I can't focus with m-my eyes open."

Artemis said, "I totally understand. I just have a couple of questions, if that's alright."

Artemis felt a strange warmth along her skin. There was no breeze coming through the open door of the house. With the screen door closed, the night air was cut off. Her hands felt clammy. And she pressed them together, if only to have something to hold on to.

She said, carefully, "I don't mean to cause any distress. Really, I don't. But I want to ask you about your cousin's death two years ago." As she said it, Artemis thought she heard movement from inside the house. For a moment, she half expected the girl's aunt to appear once more in the doorway, but nothing obstructed the light, and they were left undisturbed for the moment.

The girl shifted uncomfortably, hesitating briefly. Her fingers twitched, and Artemis spotted stains beneath the fingernails, almost the color of blood, but the texture was too thick.

Artemis hesitated, shooting a glance over her shoulder towards the garden and Forester, then, shaking her head, said, "I completely understand if you would rather not talk about it."

The girl was inhaling slowly, twisting at her sleeves. As she wrapped the elastic fabric around the finger then untangled it, Artemis noticed scars on the girl's wrists, recently healed.

She tried not to stare.

The bashful young woman was staring at the table, at the backs of her hands. She said in a mumble, "Do I have to?"

Artemis' heart went out to her. She felt a pang in her chest. She resisted the urge to glance back and look in Forester's direction, where he was still sitting on the hood of the car. Instead, she said, quietly, "You don't have to do anything you don't want to." Artemis hesitated but continued, "But there are people dying. The same age as your cousin."

Sofia shifted restlessly.

Artemis could tell by the change in her breathing tempo that she was growing nervous.

"I don't know what you want me to say. I told everything to that officer two years ago. He sat right there, in that chair."

Artemis nodded slowly. "Is it okay if you try and remember what you told him?"

The young woman looked very nervous all of a sudden. Again, she shot a look back towards the open door as if determined to run through it.

Artemis gave a quick, comforting smile. At least, she hoped it was comforting. Really, though, she felt nervous herself. Part of her was frustrated that Forester hadn't seen fit to come and help. He was the experienced interrogator. He was the agent.

"It's what I told the officer," Sofia said. "My cousin didn't commit suicide. He," she swallowed, "he was murdered."

"And how do you know that?" Artemis said.

The girl looked down, biting her lip, then looked up again. "Because," she said quietly. "I saw it happen. I was there."

Artemis went still. "Excuse me?"

Tears were now tracing Sofia's cheeks. She reached up, angrily wiping them away. "The police didn't believe me. They said I was making it up, because I spent some time in a clinic for depression a few years ago, and they knew about it. They said I was lying. He didn't even write down anything I told him."

"Who didn't?" Artemis said.

"I don't remember his name."

Artemis looked at the woman. "What did he look like?"

A shaky breath. "Bald. Big glasses."

"Ross? Do you know if his name was Detective Ross?"

The girl just shook her head, hesitant. "Maybe. I don't know."

Artemis frowned. She filed this information away for further use at a later date. Given her previous interactions with the detective, she wouldn't have been surprised if he had overlooked the testimony of a young woman deemed unreliable.

But to outright avoid taking murder claims seriously was a new level of muleheaded. Unless... there was more to the story...

Artemis said, "I know it isn't easy. But could you tell me what happened?"

The young woman shook her head. She closed her eyes. "I-I don't really remember much."

Artemis leaned in. She was trying to keep her own emotions in check but was finding it difficult.

Her heart went out to this young woman. But also, she was thinking back to the young man at the arboretum.

Artemis hesitated a moment longer then said, "Do you have a friend named John?"

The young woman frowned. "John?"

"He would work at the arboretum."

Sofia hesitated but then nodded. "I know John. I wouldn't say he's a friend. But we knew each other in school."

Artemis nodded. She felt confident now that the strange eavesdropper had been protecting Sofia. She had already been hurt. He had seemed certain that Sofia had already suffered because of this case. Artemis had thought he had meant emotional distress. But now... she could feel a slow prickle spreading along her arms.

Artemis said, adamantly, "I'm going to listen to every word. I promise. You said you were there when your cousin was murdered. Help me understand."

Sofia let out a strangled sob but inhaled and, her voice shaking, said, "He was going to kill me too."

"Excuse me?"

Sofia was practically whispering now, her arms wrapped tight around her as she said, "I really don't want to—"

"Please," Artemis insisted. "Please, try."

A strange silence had fallen over the porch.

Sofia hesitated only a moment, but then, summoning some inner resolve, she exhaled deeply and said, "I was with Jamar. We were in the gymnasium together. And then this guy came up to us. I didn't recognize him. I thought he was just another student."

"This guy was young? Could you describe him?"

"He was young. And yes, I think he had long hair. It was hard to tell. He was wearing sunglasses. But," she said, her voice shaking. "He also had a gun."

"A gun? What sort of gun?"

She hesitated. "I don't know. A handgun? He was pointing it at me and Jamar. And then, then," she said, her voice shaking. "He said something about how we were so cruel. How he was going to punish us. He said something," she hesitated, swallowed. "I don't remember the rest. But he looked very angry. I thought for sure he was going to shoot me."

"What happened next?"

Sofia let out a rattling sigh, then spoke quietly. "Jamar tried to knock the gun out of his hand. They struggled. And I ran away. I never saw him again. I thought he was right behind me," she said, her voice rising in volume. "I didn't know what happened until later that evening. I found out he was hanged. That he even left a video."

Artemis said, "Is there a chance we can see this video?"

But Sofia shook her head furiously. "I didn't keep it. His mother might have. But she's not going to give it to you."

Artemis nodded. She felt that this was an astute assumption, given her brief interaction with Sofia's aunt. "Could you describe the video to me?"

"He was saying how much he loved us. Saying that he just couldn't take it anymore. All the bullying. The cruel comments."

"Was that video recorded in the gym?"

"No. I think he made that one weeks before. I think—" she bit her lip, shot another look towards the door and kept her voice low as she said, "I think he was planning on hurting himself. But I think he changed his mind. In fact, he had fallen in love."

"He had a girlfriend?"

She nodded adamantly. "I don't know who he was dating. But it almost felt like the man with the long hair thought it was me. We tried to tell him we were cousins. But he didn't want to hear it. He kept pointing his gun at us."

Artemis frowned. "So you ran away, and then what happened—did you tell anyone?"

Here, she ducked her head and was sobbing horribly. "I didn't know what to do. I didn't have the car keys. He did. No one else was at school. I had to walk home. I tried calling my parents. But my phone died."

Artemis massaged the bridge of her nose. "Your phone was dead too?"

She paused and then let out a shaking sigh. "Not at first. I was stupid. I was trying to call my parents. I was able to place five calls. Not once did I even think to call the police, until after. I'm such an idiot. If I had just called the police, with my first call, before the phone had died, he might—" Her voice cracked again, and she began to cry, her shoulders shaking, her hands pressed to the table so tightly, it felt like she was trying to puncture the glass.

Artemis wanted to reach across the table, to console the young woman. But she also had to think analytically. Had to focus on the details. On the information. She could hear the shame. Could hear the pain. Clearly, this young woman missed her cousin.

"It's not your fault," she said, quietly. "It's not." Artemis said.

The woman didn't look up.

Artemis waited a moment, giving the young girl a second to compose herself. And then Artemis said, "Is there anything else you can tell me? Anything else about the man who was in the gym with the gun?"

Sofia hesitated but then just shook her head, her face buried in her hands. "Nothing I can think of. Nothing I remember. I don't know. I really don't know. I wish I could remember. It was all so awful."

"And the detective in charge, he didn't take any of these notes? He didn't write any of it down?"

"He," she hesitated, swallowing, "he kept asking me if I was on medicine. He was asking about the antidepressants I was taking. He made a comment about how strong the dosage was."

Artemis sighed, nodding once. She decided to reserve judgment for the moment. But she knew now she would have to speak with Detective Ross. As uncomfortable as the proposition sounded, if he had intentionally overlooked evidence, she wanted to know why. Were the police departments assigned to the case simply incompetent, or was there something nefarious under the surface?

A long-haired, young man, who looked like he could have been a senior in high school. It wasn't much of a description to go on. So far, no one involved in the case fit the description.

Artemis was struggling to keep up. There was too much information. She felt as if her mind was going haywire.

Then, quietly, she said, "Thank you for your time, Sofia. And believe me, it isn't your fault. What happened isn't your fault."

The young woman was still crying.

A shadow appeared in the doorway of the house, blocking out the stream of light. And Artemis, taking this as her cue, gave a quick nod towards Mrs. Young and then pushed away from the table, turning back towards the patio door.

There were more questions she needed to ask. Far more. But first, she needed to understand why Detective Ross had determined this woman wasn't a credible witness.

She said, carefully, "I'm going to need to speak with you again soon. Would tomorrow work?"

Sofia just shook her head and moved past her aunt in the door, disappearing into the house.

Mrs. Young was tugging at one of her curlers, trying to adjust it in her hair. She frowned at Artemis and said, "Haven't you done enough to my family?"

Then she stepped inside and slammed the door. A pause, then the sound of the chain rattling. A lock clicking into place.

Artemis sighed and turned to leave, pushing the door open.

She took the stairs on shaky legs and approached where Forester was watching her, one eyebrow raised, wearing a quizzical expression. "Well, that was interesting," he said.

"You heard all of that?"

"Most of it. I'm starting to think we should speak with Detective Ross a bit more aggressively."

Artemis nodded once. She didn't know what to make of any of it. It was starting to feel as if Ross didn't want to solve this case. And now, she was beginning to wonder if there was a more nefarious reason than pure incompetence behind this aversion to detective work.

She said, "I think that's right. And this time, you do the talking."

Forester flashed a thumbs up, swung his legs off the hood of the car, and slipped into the front seat, gesturing quickly for Artemis to join him.

It was dark again, but the night was still young.

17

Forester slammed the door to the detective's office, and Artemis nearly jumped out of her skin. She winced, rubbing a hand to her ear against the harsh sound. But her attention was quickly captured by the small, bald man, with the crimson socks, sitting in a chair at his desk; he glanced over at them, frowning. "Did Jasmine just let you waltz back in here?" Detective Ross said, pushing slowly to his feet, and as he rose from his chair, his eyebrows followed.

But Forester was shaking a finger and ended up pointing the digit at the man. "Don't try that with me—you want us to leave, you're going to have to throw us out. And in the meantime, I've got some questions I'd like to ask."

At the word *questions*, Detective Ross went still. "I answered your questions at the last crime scene as a courtesy," he said in a clipped, clear voice. "I'm beginning to think humoring you has come with a cost, and I'm not quite sure I'm willing to continue paying it." He folded his hands and then reached for a phone resting on his table.

"We know you ignored witness testimony," Artemis blurted out.

But if she had thought her outburst might affect the detective, she had been sorely mistaken. He was now pushing buttons on the phone, shaking his head as he did.

Artemis tried again, "Why did you ignore the eyewitness testimony of Ms. Perez?"

Detective Ross finished dialing the phone. He leaned slightly over, one hand keeping his suit jacket pressed against his form. "Jasmine? Send a few of the guys back here, please; I'm being harassed." He sniffed and then added, because it was in his nature to do so, "Thank you."

Then, he straightened, adjusted his suit, and frowned at the two intruders in his office. "Ms. Perez," he said slowly. "Doesn't ring any bells. Which case are we discussing now? Not that you have any say in the work this office does."

The man's face was red, his head stippled with sweat.

Artemis wasn't ready to concede the point, though. "Two years ago," she said, firmly, "Jamar Young was found hanging in a gymnasium. His cousin testified to you that it was murder. You didn't take the report."

Suddenly, Detective Ross scowled. "This is about *that* case?" He wrinkled his nose. "Don't be silly. That was an open and shut suicide."

Artemis shot Forester a look. She had insisted he take the lead, but in her eagerness to get Ross talking, she had forgotten the deal.

Forester, though, seamlessly stepped in, following her quick glance. He said, "Ms. Perez is on the record claiming it was murder."

Ross folded his arms now. Artemis thought she could hear the sound of heavy footsteps in the hall. But none of them reacted to the sound.

The detective said, "I don't remember every detail of the case, but I do remember the woman you're talking about." He leaned in now, frowning. "Did you know Ms. Perez had spent nearly two months in a psychological hospital because she was having delusional thoughts? She suffers from severe mental illness."

Artemis shot back, "What does that have to do with her testimony? She said she was with her cousin at the time of the murder."

"She said a lot of things. At one point, I'm pretty sure she said aliens had something to do with it."

Artemis started. "I find that hard to believe."

"I did too, which is why I didn't run with it. I recorded our conversation," he added quickly. "I shared it with my supervisor, and he determined I had made the right choice."

Artemis frowned. "You tossed out an entire testimony because she had spent some time at a hospital?"

"She was on heavy medications. It wasn't just some small dosage. She had filed false police claims alleging that one of the teachers at her school had attacked her cousin months before the murders. We spoke with all the students and the teacher involved. Nothing like it happened. She additionally went on to make a statement to my partner at the time, that he had been showing up in her dreams. She proceeded to say she knew my partner's future and began to describe a family, a wife, three children."

"Forester," Artemis said, slowly. She had wanted him to interject something, but instead, Forester was just watching the detective.

Ross concluded with, "The only problem, my partner at the time was single and he has never been married since. She was not reliable."

Artemis let out a long sigh; she could feel her heart pounding. While speaking with Sofia, she had felt the pain, seen it. The girl was living with her aunt, after all.

But as she considered this, she felt another rising sense of frustration. If Sofia had been making things up, then maybe Mr. Young really *had* committed suicide.

Artemis was beginning to feel like she had a headache. There were too many moving pieces. Too many things she was trying to track all at once.

She closed her eyes briefly, trying to make sense of everything she had been told.

"Another thing," said Detective Ross, now scowling at Forester. "I'm officially lodging a complaint with your department."

Artemis shifted uncomfortably in the face of the detective's threat. Forester didn't seem at all perturbed, though. Then again, she'd been the one to drag the agent into this mess. The least she could do was glean something useful.

Artemis cleared her throat delicately, and then, in a crisp, clear voice, said, "Did you have anyone in your investigation who had long, dark hair as a male teenager? He may or may not have attended Naperville Northwest."

The question had been innocuous enough. She had simply asked to cover all her bases. It was the description of the man who, delusion or not, had accosted Sofia and her cousin.

And where the question had been innocent, the reaction from the detective was startling.

His face went red, and he scowled. "Did they let you into the back? What sort of circus is this?" This last comment was muttered. He was shaking his head now in frustration.

Artemis watched the reaction, momentarily confused.

Just then, there was loud knocking on the door and gruff voices. "Detective Ross?" The door opened, and three, large police officers in uniform were standing there, frowning into the room. The man in the lead had a chest the size of a tree. His eyebrows nearly connected in the middle, and his thick, full beard was darker than his hair. The police officer glared with that impressive brow of his.

"Excuse me, but you two need to come with me," the police officer said, beckoning with an extended hand.

Forester tensed, turning surreptitiously, so his shoulders faced the approaching men.

Artemis felt a sudden shiver down her spine. "Don't. It's fine," she murmured beneath her breath at Forester. He shot her a look, raising an eyebrow.

She wasn't sure what she expected him to do. All she knew was that Forester had a punch first and ask questions later policy.

Now, the three men moved into the room, glancing towards Detective Ross as if to receive further instructions. Forester had positioned himself just a couple of inches in front of Artemis, between the approaching officers and her.

For her part, Artemis could feel her anxiety returning, but it was second to her curiosity. She tore her gaze away from the men entering the detective's office, aggression in every step and swagger. She fixed her gaze on Detective Ross, who was still scowling, a faint tinge of red covering his features.

Artemis said, slowly, "So you do know someone who fits that description?"

She didn't have to be a student of body language to know this.

But the detective was frowning; the footsteps were closer. Forester didn't budge an inch, his hands at his sides but his fingers still, his posture like a coiled spring.

"Who is it?" Artemis insisted.

Ross frowned.

"I'm just trying to help," she said, insistently. "I didn't mean to get you in trouble with anyone by talking about your private business. I'm sorry." And she meant it. She had felt bad about the way she had behaved earlier. She wasn't trying to stir the hornet's nest.

Ross, though, gave a long, shaking exhalation. He said, "Wait."

At his command, the three officers, who had reached Forester, went still. So far, no one had placed their hands on the tall, dark-haired boxer.

Forester was rolling his fingers against his thighs now, and Artemis spotted the way the twisting, white scar tissue along his palm wrapped up and around his wrist.

The three officers were glaring at Forester. Forester glared back, looking a bit like an alley cat backed into a corner.

Detective Ross didn't seem to care. "How do you know about Brent Everett?"

Artemis paused. "I didn't know that was his name. Who is he?"

The man sighed. And then, he gestured. "Come with me."

Artemis shared a look with Forester. Her partner was still busy glaring at the policeman.

But then, they stepped slowly aside at a look from the detective. Artemis and Forester, cautiously at first but picking up pace when left alone, followed Detective Ross past the three policemen and out the door. Instead of leading them towards the exit, Ross turned down the hall and began to walk briskly in another direction.

Vaguely, Artemis recognized the familiar hallway. She had been taken down this way twice in her first visit to the precinct.

They were heading to the interrogation rooms.

Artemis didn't say a word. Forester was too busy shooting threatening glances over his shoulder at the three officers who followed a few paces behind.

It was a very odd, unprofessional display if Artemis had to be honest. Then again, she hadn't spent much time around the FBI. In the movies, though, while there were often jurisdictional disputes, there was rarely the threat of having an FBI agent go hammer and tongs with three local cops in a police station.

Then again, Forester was nothing if not unpredictable.

Detective Ross reached the second metal interrogation door. He paused and shot a look back towards Artemis. He said, "Mr. Everett was a friend of Henry Rodine." Then, with a scowl, he added, "And we believe Mr. Everett and Henry made a pact. How do you know about him?"

Artemis gave a slow shake of her head.

"He was described by Ms. Perez."

If she had thought this would improve the detective's mood, she had been sorely mistaken.

He was frowning even more deeply now and hesitating outside the interrogation room. Then, he gestured at her with a cool shake of his fingers. He stood in his perfect suit and crimson socks.

As Artemis approached, carefully, he pointed through a small window in the door.

She peered through and then went still. A young man was sitting at the interrogation room table, cuffed and glaring. He had long, dark hair and a face tattoo in the shape of a spider. By the looks of things, the ink was fresh.

"That spider tattoo," detective Ross said, crisply, "only has three legs."

"Is that supposed to mean something to me?"

"We believe each leg represents a murder. We think that Mr. Everett was helping Henry in his murder spree. He's not talking but we'll get him to crack. A couple of days under pressure, and they all do eventually."

The detective gave a satisfied nod and a grunt.

And for a moment, all of them stood in the chilly hallway outside the closed, metal interrogation room door.

The floor was bright and reflective. The tiles had recently been mopped by the look of things. Even the air held a strange, clean, lemony sent.

Now, though, Artemis could feel her stomach twisting.

What were the odds that the same suspect the police were looking into for the murders fit the description that Sofia had given her?

It meant Sofia hadn't been lying. Didn't it?

Artemis hesitated, peering through the window.

"I need to speak with him," she said, suddenly.

Detective Ross frowned at her. "You will do no such thing. Do you recognize that man?"

"No," Artemis said. "But he fits a description I was given."

"I didn't think so," Ross muttered, shaking his head. "Useless... It's time for you to leave."

But Artemis shook her head again. "No, I'm sorry. I *really* need to speak with him."

She didn't try to shoulder her way through, nor did she reach for the door handle. Instead, she looked directly at Ross, her expression as sincere as she could make it. "I'm not trying to cause trouble for you, sir. I really think I might be able to help."

Ross paused. Up until this point, Artemis hadn't even considered where his younger, female partner was. In fact, Artemis hadn't seen the woman over the last hour.

She hoped her comments from earlier hadn't caused irreparable trouble.

Artemis winced at the thought. Online, playing games or commenting on a match for the sake of her audience, it was often harmless to show off a little. Now, though, she was worried she might have actually caused damage without intending to.

Detective Ross just frowned at her. He looked through the door then back at her again. "What do you think you could possibly do to help?" he said. And there was no small amount of hostility in his voice.

Artemis shook her head. "Maybe nothing. But maybe something. I know people. At least, I think I do. I want to ask him something, to clarify."

"Clarify what?"

"Something a witness told me. I might be able to put him at the scene of his first murder. Two years ago." She thought about the tragic hanging of Mr. Young. About Sofia's tears.

Artemis didn't like the idea of going behind someone's back. And in a way, by not sharing everything Sofia had said, it felt like she was undercutting the detective.

But now, something wasn't adding up. Something smelled rotten.

She frowned back towards the three police officers and then returned a look towards the detective. "Just a few minutes, and then I'll be gone. You'll never have to hear from me again."

The detective crossed his arms, closed his eyes, then said, "A few minutes. Why would I give you that? You're a civilian," he said, firmly. "However noble your intentions, I'm afraid I need to ask you, and your friend," he said, glancing at Forester, "to leave."

The way he said it left very little room for debate.

And then, Forster exclaimed, "Hey!" He whirled around with a yelp. He pointed a finger at the police officer with the impressive beard. "Pervert!" Forester yelled.

The man looked surprised, holding out his hands. "Hang on, stay back."

"You grabbed my ass," Forester yelled.

Artemis blinked in surprise.

The two other officers, who'd been glaring, went suddenly still, sharing an uncomfortable look.

"I did not," the officer yelled back.

"You did. You fondled it and everything. What's wrong with you, pervert!"

The police officer protested again, shouting his innocence.

The other cops were scowling at Forester, clearly in disbelief, but occasionally glancing towards Ross, just in case.

The detective sighed and brushed past Artemis, approaching the arguing men. "Hang on," Ross said in a placating voice. "What just happened?"

"This little pervert tried to cop a feel," Forester said. "I think he was going for the twig and berries too. He was *really* digging in there."

The officer with the beard just gaped, stammering, his cheeks turning red above his facial hair.

The other two officers took steps back, as if wanting to distance themselves as much as possible from this line of accusation.

Forester was playing it up too, wide-eyed, squawking.

But after a second, Forester shot Artemis a quick, passing look. He raised his eyebrows briefly and shot a look towards the door. And then, he started shouting, "I've never been groped by a cop before! I'm going to sue!"

The cop was still protesting his innocence. And then, when Forester kept cutting him off, the police officer started shouting, threatening him.

Still, for a brief moment as the police argued and Detective Ross tried to calm Forester, Artemis was left alone by the door of the interrogation room. She took another glance towards Forester, sighed, and then, feeling a shiver along her back, she reached out with a hand. Her fingers grazed cold metal.

No one noticed her. No one said anything. With a wince, as quietly as she could, she opened the door and pushed it with her shoulder. Still, making no noise, she slipped into the interrogation room and allowed the door to click quietly shut behind her.

She faced the suspect handcuffed at the table.

18

John wiped a hand across his forehead, leaving a streak of mud. He could feel older dirt peel from his skin from the friction, where it had mingled with sweat; he let out a long, exhausted sigh.

John lowered the pruning shears onto a hook and then adjusted a couple of the shovels that one of his coworkers had evidently placed in the wrong brackets.

He didn't complain, didn't mumble or groan as he did it. In fact, this was one of his favorite jobs he had ever had. Three years ago, the thought of having a job had been anathema to him.

But now, after a brief stint in juvenile detention, he was doing things the right way; at least, that's what his uncle said. And if there was one person John was grateful to have in his life, it was his uncle.

He paused, glancing through the small shed at the base of the hill. The arboretum had much larger tool sheds, but this one was specifically designated for newer employees.

Younger too, he supposed. The last time he had checked, he had been the youngest worker at the arboretum by nearly thirty years.

This had been another idea of his uncle's. Spending time with friends his age had been what put him behind bars.

Now, as he turned and walked out of the toolshed, he was glad to meet the night breeze, smiling at the way it refreshed him.

The breeze wafted over his skin. And ruffled his hair.

He closed the door to the shed behind him, listening as the hinges groaned. He glanced up at the small security camera placed over the door.

It didn't work. The batteries had run out nearly a month ago. Not that it mattered. He wouldn't steal from a place like this.

In fact, he was determined to never steal again.

He padlocked the door and then began marching towards the parking lot, along the small trail that carved its way through the woods.

The tree branches shook overhead, the leaves rustling on boughs.

The scent of the earth hung rich on the air.

He inhaled and gave a sigh.

As he moved away from the tools after a long day's work, he couldn't help but feel a spring in his step.

He loved the job. In fact, he couldn't think of another job he would ever want more. He didn't have as much money as he used to, when he had been on a different path. But he was far more satisfied.

It was his uncle who thought of things in the term of paths.

And now, he smiled as he considered it, he was going to stop by his girlfriend's place.

He'd been dating Sofia Perez for only a couple of months. He had never thought she would ever want to go out with him.

He still felt guilty about what had happened two years ago to her cousin.

Felt guilty about the part he had played.

But he hadn't yet found the courage to broach the subject with her.

In a way, he was scared she would never see him the same way ever again.

He frowned as he considered this and picked up his pace, heading down the trail towards the parking lot.

As he moved, though, he heard the sound of whistling wind.

He was the last of the employees at the arboretum.

A frown crept across his face.

He'd spotted a flash of light in the parking lot.

Headlights?

No one else was supposed to be here.

He paused, listening to the wind, the branches, the rustling of vegetation.

The flash of lights had vanished. Had he just been imagining things?

That's what everyone accused his girlfriend of doing. But he *believed* her. At least, he tried to.

And then he heard the sound of footsteps.

A prickle spread along his spine. He reached up, brushing his hair out of his face.

He pressed his lips tightly together, feeling the lip ring hard against his soft skin.

"Hello?" he called out into the dark.

No response.

"Hello?" he said, louder, his voice frail.

Still no response.

"Is anybody there?"

Now, he could feel his emotions beginning to rise up within him. It was hard to forget the horrible scene he'd spotted at the creek, in the normally safe arboretum.

In fact, he had been the one to discover the body. He had been the one to call the police, though, he hadn't given his name.

John had even spoken to a woman who had been there. Some sort of federal, he guessed. She had been strange, though.

Even though the FBI agent had questioned him, he hadn't said anything. Not really. Not about what he knew. Besides, if he had told them what Sofia had seen two years ago, what the police had ignored, they would have just questioned her again. And then called her crazy again. And his girlfriend was *not* crazy.

Now, though, standing alone in the dark, in the woods, he could feel his panic beginning to rise within.

Another cracking branch.

"Who's there?" he demanded.

And then a figure stepped from behind a tree onto the path.

The figure didn't say a word.

The person was wearing gloves, and there, in one hand...

They had a gun. The weapon was pointed straight at his chest.

"Wait," he yelled, desperate. "Hang on. Wait!" he shouted.

But the figure didn't flinch. Didn't move. They simply kept their weapon raised, pointed at him. He couldn't make out the person's face. They were wearing a hood, hiding their features. Then, in a whisper, voice rasping, the figure said, "We're going to go visit your girlfriend, John. If you make a sound, it will be the last thing you ever say."

19

Artemis stared at Mr. Everett, studying him. He blinked in surprise, watching where she remained by the door.

The cold air of the interrogation room caused Artemis to shiver, rubbing her hands over her arms.

She stared at the man sitting behind the table, her eyes darting to his handcuffs, and moving back to his face. He had pockmarks along his skin from old acne scars. His long, dark hair hung in clumps thanks to a combination of sweat and grease.

As she studied him, he jutted out a sharp chin beneath a protruding nose. "What are you looking at?" he snapped.

Artemis stared back then frowned deeply.

She didn't speak at first, didn't reply to the question. Preferring to watch the man who Detective Ross said had been involved with Henry.

And then, only after she considered the possibilities, feeling that strange tightness in her chest, did she say, "The going theory is that you killed our last two victims. You also had a hand, I'm guessing, in killing Henry and his girlfriend."

As she spoke, Artemis just studied him.

He didn't blink.

Just watched her, cold.

Then he said, "This is harassment. Just because I spent some time in juvie with Henry, doesn't mean I had some murder pact with the guy. I was telling your boyfriend, the bald guy with the glasses, that I didn't do anything."

Artemis watched him. "That's not what Ms. Perez tells us," she said slowly.

As she talked, Artemis realized she was playing a game that she didn't quite know how to win. Revealing information to a suspect, names, was probably not the best way to approach this.

But she had decided on a calculated risk.

She needed to see his reaction at Sofia's name.

Not because she thought this man was guilty.

That didn't make sense. No, she had already decided, it was too much of a coincidence.

What were the odds that the man who Sofia Perez had just told Artemis about was sitting in the interrogation room right as she had gotten back? No—rather, Artemis felt there was a much more obvious explanation.

She watched closely and realized, the moment she said Sofia's name, that she had been wrong.

He didn't flinch. Didn't blink. Didn't frown. In fact, there was nearly no reaction whatsoever.

She might as well have simply said nothing.

Sofia's name clearly wasn't familiar to the man.

People could play at disguising their reactions.

In fact, some people were very good at it.

But Artemis prized herself on being able to read others. And this wasn't someone with a poker face; he was still sneering, contemptuous of her. Angry, frustrated.

And Sofia's name didn't matter.

So she tried again, "Did you have anything to do with the murder of Jamar Young?"

Now he didn't react. He wrinkled his nose. "You're joking?"

She shook her head, still watching him.

"That kid killed himself. Everyone knows it."

She felt a faint shiver along her arms. She nodded slowly. "So I've been told."

He wrinkled his nose. "It's true. Everyone knows it's true."

Artemis said, quietly, "So you're saying you didn't kill Mr. Young?"

He scoffed. "You sound like that stupid whore."

Artemis didn't react at the insult. "Like who?"

"The chick that's been sending those threatening messages. Man, she doesn't scare me. Was that you? Cops trying to scare me into a confession? Well, I didn't do it. He killed himself. Everyone knows it. He just couldn't take the heat. That's his own damn fault."

Artemis frowned.

"Besides, Henry was the cruel one. I just teased a little. Everyone did. Wasn't my fault that Henry took that video."

Artemis felt the slow prickle return to her arms. "What video?"

"The one of him in the bathroom stall. He was looking at pictures of some of the girls in school. Pictures he took. Henry filmed him and showed everyone. The kid was so embarrassed, he killed himself. Not that we missed him. No one cared. Only that creepy cousin of his. Wait, Perez. Hold on. That was her name, wasn't it? What's she been saying?" He smirked now, leaning back, oily, greasy hair framing his face.

But Artemis was trying to piece it all together. She stared at the belligerent man. But as she did, her eyes narrowed.

"You're saying Henry posted a video of Jamar Young in the bathroom?"

"Yeah. It was kind of funny. He added captions and everything." Everett chuckled, bobbing his head. "You should've seen it."

Artemis hesitated. And then she said, "And who all saw it? Who all commented on it?"

"Commented? I don't know. It was mostly just the school. It's not like the thing went viral or anything. A couple of hundred people saw it. Maybe twenty commented. Some other schools in the area too, I guess. I don't know, just mostly guys in the area. People who saw the video. What more do you want?"

Artemis, though, had turned her back. She was moving towards the door.

Suddenly, the door was flung open, and she found herself standing face to face with a scowling Detective Ross.

"Get out," he said, his voice harsh. "Get out, or I'm going to arrest you."

Artemis nodded quickly. She sidled past Ross.

Forester was waiting at the end of the hall.

Before Ross could change his mind, Artemis hurried, picking up her pace and moving towards the tall agent.

The three police officers were still lining the hall, frowning at Artemis, and scowling at Forester.

Artemis ducked her head, keeping her eyes on the ground, moving swiftly.

"Get out of the precinct. Get out of my town!" Ross shouted after them. Done was his docile, calm nature. Gone was his attempt at playing nice.

Now, he just sounded furious.

Artemis didn't look back. Didn't glance at the police officers. She approached Forester, quickly. Then, beneath her breath, she said, "It's not him. He didn't do it."

Forester turned with her, falling into step and marching back towards the exit. "You're sure?" he said quietly.

"A hundred percent," she said firmly. "He didn't do it. But I think I know who did. And I think I know why. I need you to drive me again."

But Forester didn't protest. He just nodded, took it in stride, and picked up the pace, moving with her towards the sliding, glass doors of the police precinct.

20

Artemis slammed the car door, taking the stairs to the patio two at a time. When she reached the glass door, she didn't hesitate but instead swung it open, stepped past the table, and began pounding her fist on the wooden door to Mrs. Young's house.

This time, Forester didn't wait at the bottom of the stairs but instead joined her, also pounding his fist against the door.

"Mrs. Young?" Artemis shouted. "Open the door, please."

She glanced towards the window. The lights were off. She didn't stop, continuing to slam her fist.

Forester was watching her out of the corner of his eye. On the drive over, she had given muted, hesitant answers, running over the clues as best she could. This was the only thing that made sense.

Sometimes things that were coincidences, were orchestrated.

She pounded louder.

A few seconds passed.

Forester said, quietly, "So, explain to me again why you think it's her?"

Before she could reply, the door suddenly rattled. The sound of the chain being unhooked. A lock being turned. A few seconds passed, and then the door opened.

There, glaring out at them, still wearing her hair curlers and bathrobe, Mrs. Young frowned towards the two figures standing on her porch.

"What in the world are you doing?" she said. "Are you trying to wake the dead?"

Artemis, though, shook her head. Her tone was urgent, her voice shaking. "Where's your niece?"

"Sofia? In her room."

"Please take me to her."

But here, Mrs. Young scowled.

Forester, though, flashed his badge this time. He said, in a gruff, authoritative voice, "We need to speak with your niece, ma'am."

For a moment, Artemis thought she might refuse.

So Artemis said, quickly, "I have reason to believe she's putting herself in danger."

Artemis didn't add the second part. That she also had reason to believe someone else was in danger.

But at these words, Mrs. Young hesitated. "In danger? How would she be in danger?"

The woman shot a panicked glance over Artemis' shoulder, glancing towards the street.

But there were no cars. No one else walking along the sidewalks. No lights in the homes across the street.

Still, Mrs. Young glanced back at Artemis, her voice shrill. "What danger?"

Artemis wasn't sure what it felt like to lose a son. She had lost a sister, though. It hurt to this day.

But she didn't have time for more than a sympathetic nod. "Please, take us to your niece. I need to speak with her."

Mrs. Young didn't seem swayed by Forester's badge. But the earnest tone Artemis communicated with seemed to do it.

Her concern for her niece prompted her to push the door open a bit wider, step back, and point to Forester. "Outside, unless you have a warrant. You, come with me." She made a crook of her finger, wiggling it and indicating Artemis.

Forester didn't protest. He waited in the door and shrugged at Artemis.

She hadn't told him her full suspicions. If she had, she doubted Forester would have been willing to stay behind. But for the moment, she'd gotten what she needed.

And so, with a quick nod, Artemis followed Mrs. Young into her home. They passed a coat rack where a few hats dangled.

Mrs. Young walked with a bit of a limp, moving through her house, in the dark. Old, wooden floorboards creaked as she moved. She was shaking her head and muttering, "Never in all my years..."

Artemis didn't speak, preferring to follow the woman. They came to a stop in front of a room at the end of the hall. The door had butterflies on the front and also a metal sign which read *Keep Out*.

Artemis waited patiently.

Mrs. Young knocked.

No reply.

The woman knocked louder. "Sofia! I know you don't like being bothered in your room, but I have that FBI lady back to speak with you. Sofia?"

Artemis felt the prickle spreading. She'd been right. She knew she'd been right.

Mrs. Young tentatively turned the handle and pushed open the door.

Artemis stared into the bedroom. The bed was empty—a window was open, left cracked.

Mrs. Young hesitated, glancing around the room. "That's strange," she said slowly. "I was just in the bathroom. She's not there."

The woman frowned, and Artemis could see the blood beginning to drain from her face, her cheeks turning pale.

"Sofia?" Mrs. Young called out, trying to keep her voice steady but struggling to do so.

Artemis, glanced around the room once more, shot a look towards the door they had passed which led to the bathroom.

And then, she said, "Stay here, Mrs. Young. Lock your doors."

And then Artemis turned and broke into a jog. She shot a couple of cursory glances in the rooms she passed. But she knew there was no point.

Sofia wasn't here.

She raced towards Forester, pushing out of the front door, and, breathing heavily, beneath her breath, she said, her voice urgent, "Sofia is the killer."

"How can you be sure?" Forester shot back, also quiet.

Artemis shook her head. "I'm at least eighty-percent sure. I'll tell you on the way. We need to go. *Now.*"

"Go where?"

"To speak with the one person who was trying to protect her!"

Forester was moving out too, quickening his pace to keep up. "The kid at the Arboretum?"

Artemis nodded adamantly. "She had dirt beneath her fingernails."

"Excuse me?"

193

Artemis shot a look across the hood of the car, one hand braced against the door. "The wrong color dirt. It doesn't match her aunt's flowerbeds and I saw that same type of dirt back at the Arboretum. It didn't make sense to me at first. But now it does. I think she's going back. John—"

"Who's John?"

"The kid who spoke to me there. John said he was working late. Come on, Forester. We need to hurry. And I mean fast."

Artemis was shaking so badly it took her a second to open the door.

Forester, though, had hands as steady as stone. He didn't look anxious, or nervous. If anything, he seemed excited as he slipped into his car, and Artemis followed.

She shot a look towards the door, where Mrs. Young was standing, staring dazedly out after them.

Artemis wasn't sure how much the woman had heard.

Her heart broke for Mrs. Young. But right now, she felt almost certain that John was in danger.

21

Artemis stared through the windshield, willing Forester to go faster. She could just glimpse the tops of the trees in the Arboretum as they rounded the intersection, cutting across two lanes and over yellow painted lines.

No one was on the street to honk at them.

Forester gripped the steering wheel, guiding them up the entrance, into the arboretum.

"He said he worked late," Artemis was saying. "I wish I'd asked how late. What if he isn't here?"

Forester, frowning, shooting a look in her direction. "Tell me again why you think Sofia is the killer?"

Artemis said, firmly, "Because she told me that a man fitting Mr. Everett's description held her at gunpoint."

"I thought you said that was because she was delusional."

"That's what Detective Ross said. But she told me something different than what she told Ross."

Forester shot her a quick glance. "What do you mean?"

"Ross mentioned something about blaming aliens for her cousin's death. But she only mentioned a person to me. And it just so happened *that person* was someone who taunted her cousin online. Who mocked him for a video that Henry uploaded?"

Forester stared. "You think she's targeting people who made fun of her cousin? Why?"

Artemis said, her voice shaky, "Because I really do think he killed himself. She calls it murder because she really believes it is. She believes that their harassment led her cousin to kill himself."

Forester pulled into the parking lot of the arboretum. There was a chain blocking two posts. But the chain had been snapped. Artemis could see a car, parked haphazardly across two painted lines, one wheel resting on top of the shattered chain.

"They're here," she said, urgently. "Forester, we have to hurry. I think she's going to kill John."

"The arboretum worker? Why?"

"I don't know. But she wanted us to think that Mr. Everett had something to do with it. She was trying to frame him. Whatever her vendetta, she will go to whatever lengths it takes."

Forester frowned but pushed out of the vehicle and glanced at the broken chain and the poorly parked sedan.

Artemis could feel her pulse quickening. The dirt was one clue. Bringing up someone that just so happened to be a suspect the police were looking into suggested that Sofia had known who the detectives were looking into.

Henry clearly had a record of taunting, threatening, bullying.

And sometimes, people who were picked on could join the crowd. She thought of Kyler in the other video where Henry was seen threatening him.

Just because someone was a victim, didn't mean they weren't also someone else's perpetrator.

They were just pieces. Scattered pieces—nothing concrete. Nothing clear.

But Sofia had lied about her experience. Her cousin had killed himself.

And she blamed the people who had taunted him, who had watched that video Henry had taken. Henry had a habit of taking offensive videos. First with Kyler in the bleachers. Then with the one Everett mentioned.

Sofia had been terrified, panicked when Artemis had spoken with her. But what if that hadn't been out of PTSD but out of fear of being interrogated by someone with the FBI?

The sort of fear that a guilty party might experience.

Artemis frowned, hastening after Forester. She stepped over the shattered chain, skirting the parked sedan.

Another car was parked closer to a trail.

Forester was frowning, glancing along two branching paths.

There was the Eastern Trail, which completed a three-mile loop. And the Western Trail, which went on for eight miles and included a small pond.

Artemis stared.

Forester said, "Which one should we go down first?"

"There's no time," Artemis said, urgently. "We can't wait. We have to go down both."

Forester wrinkled his nose. "I already called for backup. They're going to be a while, Artemis. I'm not sending you off alone."

But she shook her head, already moving. Even after taking a couple of steps, she paused, breathing shakily. She closed her eyes, steadying her mind, then with a quick nod, she picked up her pace again, hastening up the western path.

Forester came after her, following. She turned sharply. "No!"

"What do you mean *no.*"

"They're here, Forester. They're here somewhere. If I'm heading in the wrong direction, she could *kill* him."

Forester let out a puff of air. He raised his phone as if checking something, shook his head and glanced over his shoulder towards the park's entrance. Far in the distance, Artemis thought she heard the wail of sirens. She frowned, though, returning her attention to the FBI agent. She didn't want to say it, didn't want to insist.

She didn't like the idea of wandering through the woods on her own.

Forester, though, gave her a final look, then said. "Fine, but you're taking this."

He reached towards his leg, pulled up his pants and snatched a small, ankle firearm. He handed it to her, pressing it against her fingers. "That's the safety. Aim; pull the trigger. Simple as that."

Artemis swallowed, staring at the weapon.

So far, she'd refused to take a gun when consulting with the FBI. She simply couldn't bring herself to use it.

Didn't see the point. Guns made her uncomfortable, anyhow.

Now, though, Forester pressed the weapon against her palm, curled her fingers and patted twice. Then, he stepped back, staring at her. The tall man's shadow stretched towards her, across the ground. She inhaled softly, staring back at him.

He didn't flinch. Didn't move. Just watched, as if waiting to see how serious she was.

Artemis shot another glance over her shoulder, towards the trees, along the dusty, dirt-strewn path. No sounds. No indication that anyone had gone that way. No sign anyone had gone along the other, longer path either, though.

Artemis regarded the oddly parked car, frowning. Part of her wished the vehicle itself might provide a clue.

But no.

She sighed and then turned, beginning to walk quickly. She didn't say another word but began to pick up the pace. Her hand sweated where she gripped the weapon. Her heart pounded horribly. She began to move quicker, faster.

And then, she heard a sigh, a grunt, and the sound of retreating footsteps as Forester went in the opposite direction, checking the second trail.

Only after the sound of his footsteps faded did Artemis pause long enough to feel a shiver down her spine. She frowned, standing beneath the whispering branches, the shivering leaves. Inhaling the odor of earth and stream-water. The scent of the surrounding forest.

She tried to peer through the dark, but there was no movement. No sound.

What if she'd sent Forester in the wrong direction?

She gritted her teeth, forcing the thought aside, and breaking into a dead sprint.

She raced forward now, kicking up dust, and occasionally inhaling so sharply, she tasted the particles of dirt on her tongue. She spat as she hastened forward, crossing a small bridge over a flow of water.

Ahead, the trees were thicker, wider, the branches stubbier, the roots stumpy. She kept going, searching one way then the other, trying to listen even above the sound of her own panting, of her rapid footfalls.

Artemis was mostly certain she'd been right.

Mostly certain that Sofia had been lying.

The coincidence had been too contrived. The dirt beneath the fingernails had stood out. And she wasn't in her room.

Artemis shook her head fiercely, sprinting now, arms pumping.

But as she raced along the trail, breathing heavily, she couldn't help but feel a slow, dawning sense of fear.

What if she was wrong?

What if she was heading in the wrong direction?

She cursed, slowing for a moment, allowing the wind to caress her, to toss her hair, to ruffle her clothing. As she came to a stop in the center of the road, glancing one way then the other, she froze. She inhaled shakily, swallowing.

Silence.

Only the trees. The creak, the groan, the shiver, the shudder...

Only the woods...

She'd chosen the wrong path.

She shot a look back over her shoulder. The path looped around, heading the other direction. Though she couldn't see the road from here, she knew the asphalt of the second, looping road couldn't have been more than a hundred paces away.

She hesitated, wondering if she ought to sprint back towards where—

"*Help!*"

She froze, staring ahead, startled like a doe.

Another shout, this one strangled, though, desperate and suddenly cut off.

Her heart pounded and her breath came quickly. She swallowed and stared towards the trees. And then she heard the sound of a voice. The cracking of twigs. The sound of desperate gasping.

Artemis bolted forward, her small weapon clutched in hand.

The safety was... which part? Shit. She hadn't been looking.

No—no, she could figure this out. There... was that? No...

That? *Click.*

Something fell out of the bottom of the gun. She cursed, stumbling to a halt, kicking up leaves now that had scattered across the trail.

A small clip of bullets had been ejected.

"Shit. Shit." She bent, snatched the clip, slipped it back in place, pushed.

And then, careful not to lose her only defensive option, she raced forward. She didn't shout. Didn't scream out for Forester. Didn't know if any sound would only spook the killer.

Artemis hastened forward, heart pounding, footsteps desperate.

And then she came to a stumbling halt, staring down an incline, her eyes the size of saucers.

"You think I dated you because I *like* you?" a voice demanded, scorn seeping from the words. "I *know* what you said to him! I saw it, John! I saw it all. Now stop it and put it over your neck. Do it or I'll shoot you in the leg! I mean it!"

Artemis felt her pulse racing.

Two figures were facing each other at the bottom of a small, grassy incline. The first thing Artemis spotted was the gun clutched in Sofia's hand, pointed directly towards John's chest. He was standing on the log, shifting uncomfortably. A rope taut in his hands, a noose draped over his head like a halo, but he hadn't yet lowered it onto his shoulders.

Sofia was waving her gun now, insistently.

"Do it, John!" she yelled.

He was crying though, shaking his head, tears streaking his cheeks and standing out like frost. "Why?" he said. "I thought you loved me!"

"Love you?" she yelled. And then in a rage, she raised her phone, cleared her throat and began to read. "*Hahaha! Look at that creepy, little pervert. I hope he chokes tonight! Weird freak!*" She looked up, her lips tight. "Remember that?" she murmured. "Because I do. Jamar remembered it too. He *killed* himself. That was your post... it was the nicest one, too. You should have seen what Henry posted. What Kyler said. What Lucy wrote. Is it funny now?" she asked, stepping forward suddenly and jamming her gun against him. "What? No more *hahaha*! Put the noose on. NOW!" She screamed with such force that Artemis winced as she slipped from tree to tree, racing down the incline.

Still crying, John slowly lifted the noose, placing it over his head, pulling it like a sweater neck and wrapping it around his throat.

"Stop blubbering!" Sofia snapped. "That didn't stop you guys from taunting him, did it? Jamar never hurt *anyone!* But you guys wanted him dead!"

Artemis came closer, raising her gun now, her breath coming in puffs. As she drew nearer, nearer still, in slow, shuffling movements, Sofia began to reach out, placing a hand in the center of John's chest, preparing to shove him off his precarious purchase.

But as she made to push, Artemis suddenly shouted.

"Don't!" She had her gun raised now, pointing down the incline.

Sofia whirled around, her own weapon raised.

The two women stared at each other, both of them breathing rapidly, both of them with weapons raised.

"Get back!" Sofia said, her voice shaking. "Go away!"

Artemis stepped closer, still gripping her gun. She still didn't know if the safety was on or off. She felt a flare of frustration.

Sofia was shaking now, trembling. "I—I don't want to hurt you! This doesn't involve you!"

"Help!" John tried to shout.

"Shut up," Sofia snarled, half-turning to face him again.

Artemis yelled to distract the younger woman. "Hey! Hey—Sofia, don't!" she said, her voice firm. She wished she felt *half* as strong as she moved slowly down the grassy incline, only twenty paces away. Fifteen. Ten...

She drew closer, her heart hammering, her gun trembling where she gripped it.

Forester was nowhere in sight. Even if he'd heard them, he would have been heading the opposite direction at this point. Artemis came to a stop, weapon clutched, her breath coming in rapid pants.

Sofia wasn't *quite* aiming at Artemis. The girl was clearly scared.

"You killed them," Artemis said, quietly. "You made them hang themselves then shot the girlfriends."

"They murdered Jamar!" she screamed. "They murdered him! Go away! Let me do this. I'm going to end what they started... Don't worry, you won't have to shoot me." Her hand was shaking so badly, she nearly dropped the gun.

Artemis just stared, resisting the urge to close her eyes in exhaustion. In grief.

"They posted things about Jamar, is that right?" Artemis said quietly. "Your cousin?"

Sofia was crying now too, and John—still on the log—was on his tiptoes, struggling to grip the rope around his neck. "They wanted him to die!" she screamed. "They were merciless! Y-you should have seen some of the things they wrote! No shame—no... no decency!" Her eyes flashed now, she snarled. "So I killed them! I almost killed myself, you know. When I found him, two years ago, I saw him hanging from the basketball hoop! I did—*me!*" She was now waving her gun around, her tears replaced by snarls and scoffing. "I almost killed myself... but..." She swallowed. "But..."

"He wasn't just your cousin, was he?" Artemis said quietly, feeling a slow flicker of realization. This had been the part she'd been missing. The motive. Why boyfriend and girlfriend? Why attack both?

And now it made sense. Even as she asked, she spotted the grief in the young woman's eyes.

"We're not blood! We... we *weren't!*" she exclaimed, her voice hoarse. "We *weren't*. He loved me!" she sobbed. "And I loved him. They had no right to take him. None! And so I did the same!" she yelled now, spittle flying as she rounded on John once more. "You think I liked you? When you kissed me, my skin crawled! But you—you're the last piece, John. You and me. Tonight. We're both going to meet our friends. I hope to see you in hell!"

She raised her weapon, aimed.

Artemis yelled. But she didn't try to fire. Didn't know how—didn't have the instinct.

Instead of shooting, though, she jabbed her gun forward, *hard*. Artemis yelled as John was knocked off the log. He started kicking, writhing mid-air, trying to speak, to gasp, his fingers clutching at the rope taut around his neck.

At the same time, Sofia kicked the log and then turned and ran, sprinting into the woods. Artemis bolted forward, racing across the grass, lunging towards the gasping arboretum worker. His hands groped at the rope, wrapped taut around his neck and attached to a tree branch above.

Artemis held on as tightly as she could, arms wrapped around his waist, lifting with a groan. She could hear the rapid sound of footfalls as Sofia raced towards the looping path which led *back* towards the parking lot.

Artemis' arms strained. She wasn't a particularly, physically *strong* woman. She spent most of her nights studying positions and openings. But now, she held out as tightly as she could, trying her best to lift him up.

But try as she might, heaving as she did, John was too heavy for her. She could hear him gasping still, desperate, kicking.

She could only think of one solution.

Artemis pulled the gun she had, shouted, "Hold onto the rope, tight! Now!" and stepped back. She aimed, unsure if the safety was still on or off.

She pointed at the rope, far enough over John's head that she wasn't risking him, and then fired.

Missed.

Fired again.

Missed again.

She cursed, stepping closer, on her tiptoes, trying to touch the rope with the gun. John was still gagging, kicking, lashing out and using her shoulder to push himself up.

She aimed and fired twice more.

The rope frayed. Frayed again...

Then, another kick from John...

The rope snapped.

He collapsed to a heap on the ground, gasping, fingers scrabbling at the rope wrapped taut.

Artemis dropped to his side, pulling the noose off his neck. "Are you okay?" she said desperately. "Are you alright?"

"Artemis!" she heard a voice from further down the trail. "Artemis!"

"Forester!" she shouted. "Here! We need paramedics!"

John was breathing though, clutching at his neck, tears streaming down his face but very much alive. She winced, patted him on the arm, but then spun on her heel. She just glimpsed the form of Sofia sprinting along the path, racing back towards the parking lot.

Artemis pointed now. "There! Forester!"

But the tall agent was racing straight towards her.

Artemis hissed in frustration. Forester wasn't paying attention. He was racing down the path on the opposite loop just as Sofia crossed the same point on the parallel road.

Artemis made a split-second decision. "You're going to be okay," she murmured, adding another comforting pat, and then she broke into a sprint, racing down the hill in the direction of Sofia's fleeing form. Her footsteps pounded the ground, and she hopped over another toppled log strewn with lichen and moss.

After a few steps, she realized she was still gripping her gun. Artemis raced down the hill, faster, heart pounding. This wasn't what she was cut out for. She wasn't an action hero. Wasn't meant to go racing through the woods in pursuit of some killer... but if she didn't...

Sofia was going to kill herself. That much was obvious. She also could be a danger to others... *Shit.*

Forester was close, but he saw the fallen victim and, with a curse, dropped to John's side. "Artemis!" he yelled. "Wait!"

But she didn't. She sprinted through the woods and finally hit the path. Ahead, she spotted the flare of a car's headlights.

She didn't stop though, still running. Very much feeling out of her depth.

Artemis raced into the parking lot, gasping, sweating, her gun in one hand. Sofia was sitting in her vehicle, eyes wide in panic, desperately trying to start her car.

But Artemis didn't wait. She rushed forward.

Sofia started the engine. It roared to life and began to pull away.

Artemis reached out, snatching at the door handle, dragged along a few paces as she pulled the door open while the car was still picking up speed. With a gasp, she flung herself into the back seat, deciding this would give her a better angle than the front. Sofia yelped at the sound of the slamming door, eyes darting to the mirror. She cursed, trying to reach for her gun, but as she did, the vehicle began to veer off the road.

Artemis yelled, her adrenaline racing now. She wasn't even sure what she was doing. All she knew was that she couldn't let this woman get away.

Sofia's weapon was on the seat next to her. Artemis lunged at it first. Sofia snatched Artemis' wrist.

Instead of continuing for the gun, though, Artemis jerked her hand *back,* yanking Sofia's arm with her. Again, the steering wheel veered, the car rolled off the side of the road.

Sofia yelled, Artemis braced, and the car slammed into a tree.

It was moving slowly, though, and didn't even shatter the windshield as it came to a jarring halt.

Artemis' head bounced off the seat. Sofia hit the horn, sending a blaring sound. And then the two women struggled. Artemis tried to hold Sofia. But she kept trying to get away.

Artemis gasped and hyperventilated with the desperate scramble for control. From the back seat, her arms were wrapping around Sofia's own arm, her neck, trying to hold her back. Sofia, meanwhile, was crying, struggling, scratching. She wanted nothing more than to get away.

Artemis wanted nothing more than to hold on.

Vaguely, even in the chaos, the desperation, thoughts of Helen surfaced.

Artemis wasn't willing to give up most things without a fight.

More scraping of fingernails along her skin. Artemis winced as the nails drew blood. She gasped, holding tight, yelling incoherently in Sofia's ear. She held tight, refusing to give in. Sofia was beginning to lose steam. She was crying, trying to reach for the gun on the seat then trying to snatch at Artemis.

But from behind, Artemis had the advantage.

She held on as if her life depended on it. There was little else she could do.

"Let go!" Sofia was saying. "Let go!"

In the distance now, Artemis could hear sirens rapidly approaching.

"P-please," Sofia begged. "Let go!"

But Artemis kept her grip. One hand wrestling Sofia's shooting hand. Her other arm holding Sofia's head back against the headrest, wrapped around the woman's neck.

Artemis didn't think she could overpower anyone physically. That wasn't what she brought to the table.

She just had to last long enough...

Long enough until...

Flashing lights appeared at the arboretum road.

Forester was shouting, sprinting from the path. "Hands up!" he yelled. "Get your hands up!"

Sofia screamed in desperation, lunging for the gun a final time, but Artemis beat her to it, knocking the weapon onto the floor.

And only then, as police converged, as lights flashed and Forester yelled...

Only then did Sofia go limp, shaking horribly, tears streaming down her face.

And even then, her arm aching, Artemis didn't let go.

EPILOGUE

Artemis smiled in the direction of Mrs. Washington's small, pink car. The woman waved a final time as she pulled away from the curb outside the airport. Her husband Henry sat in the back seat. He also gave a small wave, but his hand moved slowly. His heart didn't seem in it.

Still, he was out of the house.

Cynthia had whispered, on their way to the airport, this was because of Artemis clearing their grandson's name.

Cynthia leaned out the window, gesturing one last time. Artemis took a step forward, smiling.

"Thank you, dear," Mrs. Washington said, her eyes shining bright, her lips pressed in a thin line. Her expression matched the tone of Jamie Kramer from his voicemail. A tone of inevitability.

Artemis nodded quickly. "You're very welcome, ma'am." A car behind them was honking, trying to usher the Washingtons out of the yellow marked parking slot.

Cynthia sighed, glancing in the mirror, but returned her attention to Artemis. "If you ever need anything," she said quietly, her eyebrows inching up on her forehead. "I really mean it. You... you're a true friend, Ms. Blythe."

Artemis smiled, leaning in and pressing her hand against Cynthia's.

The car horn behind them blared.

Flustered, Mrs. Washington put the car in gear, waved again and began to pull back into the flow of traffic moving past the terminals.

For a moment, as she left, waving again, Artemis felt a surge of guilt. She'd told Mrs. Washington that her grandson hadn't been the killer... But Artemis hadn't told Cynthia what other things she'd found out about Henry. She sighed. Then again, what would the point have been?

She stood on the curb outside the airport, exhaling slowly, closing her eyes for a moment. It wasn't so much to savor diesel fuels and the dulcet tones of airport traffic.

More like, she needed a moment to let her choice settle.

She felt her nerves returning, but even these couldn't distract her from the gravity of the situation. The small, pink car was pulling away now, vanishing. An elegant hand was extended out the window, waving one last time. Artemis raised her own hand, fingers spread, then lowered it again, feeling a wave of melancholy.

She hated goodbyes.

Artemis glanced at her phone, hefting her laptop bag, and closing her eyes. Then, she turned slowly to face the airport doors. She raised the phone.

And as she began to move, she made a call.

The phone rang as she entered the airport frowning.

Forester was taking a later flight. Artemis suspected he simply didn't want to face Agent Grant so soon. But also, he was sticking around to help with the interrogation process. To find out *exactly* why Sofia had done what she had.

Artemis wanted no part of it.

She knew why the girl had killed. She knew that type of grief.

She thought of the Dawkins. Thought of the other folk back in Pinelake. How often had she sometimes wondered what it might feel like to get revenge against the people who had treated her like a pariah all those years?

She sighed slowly, moving into the airport. Then again, not everyone back home was like that...

Home.

What a strange notion.

The phone connected.

A cool, crisp voice. "Hello?"

"Agent Grant?"

"Artemis."

"I... I wanted to speak with you..."

"You're accepting the offer."

Artemis paused, frowning at her flight, at the top of the departures board behind baggage-check. *Seattle. On-time.*

She sighed.

The case with Henry hadn't turned out how she'd wanted. But she'd made an oath. She'd solved the case.

Which meant... perhaps...

If she was unwilling to let go...

Maybe there was a chance Helen was still out there. And even if not...

Did she want to know the truth? What had really happened seventeen years ago? Artemis hadn't given Mrs. Washington the *full* truth about her grandson. But she'd given the part that mattered.

Henry wasn't a murderer.

But Artemis' father *was*. Her sister, though, was dead... At least, that's what she'd thought for years. But was it possible she was still alive?

Possible.

Artemis cleared her throat, shouldering her bag. "I'd like to accept your offer," Artemis said quietly. "I'm flying in tonight."

Agent Grant hesitated a moment. Cleared her throat. Then said, "Good. Because I already have your rental."

"My what?"

"Agency provides certain benefits, Ms. Blythe. I've been expecting this call. We'll sort out the details later. I'll send Wade to pick you up from the airport."

Artemis closed her eyes without replying, breathing slowly. Was this the right choice? Or was she making a mistake?

Her father was back in the Pacific Northwest...

People who hated her lived near Seattle.

Her brother was there too... and so was Jamie Kramer.

Artemis sighed. And then said, in as articulate a tone as she could manage, "Thank you, Agent Grant. I'll see you soon."

And then she hung up and approached the airport counter.

In a way, it didn't *quite* feel like turning a new page.

More like... starting an entirely new story.

Artemis Blythe, the Ghostkiller's daughter, was heading home. As she stood at the counter, her eyes darted to a small wire rack near a juice shop set in the opposite wall. She hesitated, glancing over, and then went still.

The wire rack was covered in postcards.

Some of the postcards she recognized.

She stared at the cards, then stared at the juice bottles on the shelf behind them. Then at the cards again. And suddenly, a slow, sickly sense of realization twisted in her gut.

"Holy shit..." she muttered, turning away from the counter and staring at the cards.

It suddenly made sense. It *clicked* into place. She'd ruled out the other options... leaving her with an entirely new possibility.

And there, staring at the rack, she realized what her father had been up to. What Baker had been doing by sending those postcards to her father. They weren't notes... They weren't messages.

They were bribes.

She turned sharply, pulling her phone from her pocket.

The End

WHAT IS NEXT FOR ARTEMIS?

SHE'S BURIED DEEP

A homecoming baptized in bones...

Artemis Blythe has returned to her old stomping grounds, this time as an official consultant of the FBI. And this new case will be like none other. A mass grave is found in the mountains. The bones of long forgotten victims hidden in a mine shaft.

The mountains outside Pinelake are combed for more victims.

And then another mass grave is found.

And another.

And while Artemis sets out with Agents Grant, Forester and Wade to solve the old cases, she's faced with a spine-chilling thought. What if some of these bones belong to her sister? Helen disappeared around the same time as these graves were formed.

In a twist, Artemis is forced to confront old fears in a race against the clock to find the most prolific serial killer she's ever heard of.

And through it all... she can only hope...

Her sister Helen isn't identified among the slain.

WANT TO KNOW MORE?

Greenfield press is the brainchild of bestselling author Steve Higgs. He specializes in writing fast paced adventurous mystery and urban fantasy with a humorous lilt. Having made his money publishing his own work, Steve went looking for a few 'special' authors whose work he believed in.

About the Author

Georgia Wagner

Georgia Wagner worked as a ghost writer for many, many years before finally taking the plunge into self-publishing. Location and character are two big factors for Georgia, and getting those right allows the story to flow seamlessly onto the page. And flow it does, because Georgia is so prolific a new term is required to describe the rate at which nerve-tingling stories find their way into print.

When not found attached to a laptop, Georgia likes spending time in local arboretums, among the trees and ponds. An avid cultivator of orchids, begonias, and all things floral, Georgia also has a strong penchant for art, paintings, and sculptures. A many-decades long passion for mystery novels and years of chess tournament experience makes Georgia the perfect person to pen the Artemis Blythe s

Printed in Great Britain
by Amazon